LEGACY OF LIMGA

Sequel to Marranga Limga

FAYE ROOTS

Published in the United States of America

ISBN 978-1-970703-36-8 (Paperback)

ISBN 978-1-970703-37-5 (Hardback)

ISBN 978-1-970703-38-2 (eBook)

For Book Rights Adaption and other Rights Permission.

Call us at toll-free **601-914-6178**.

Contents

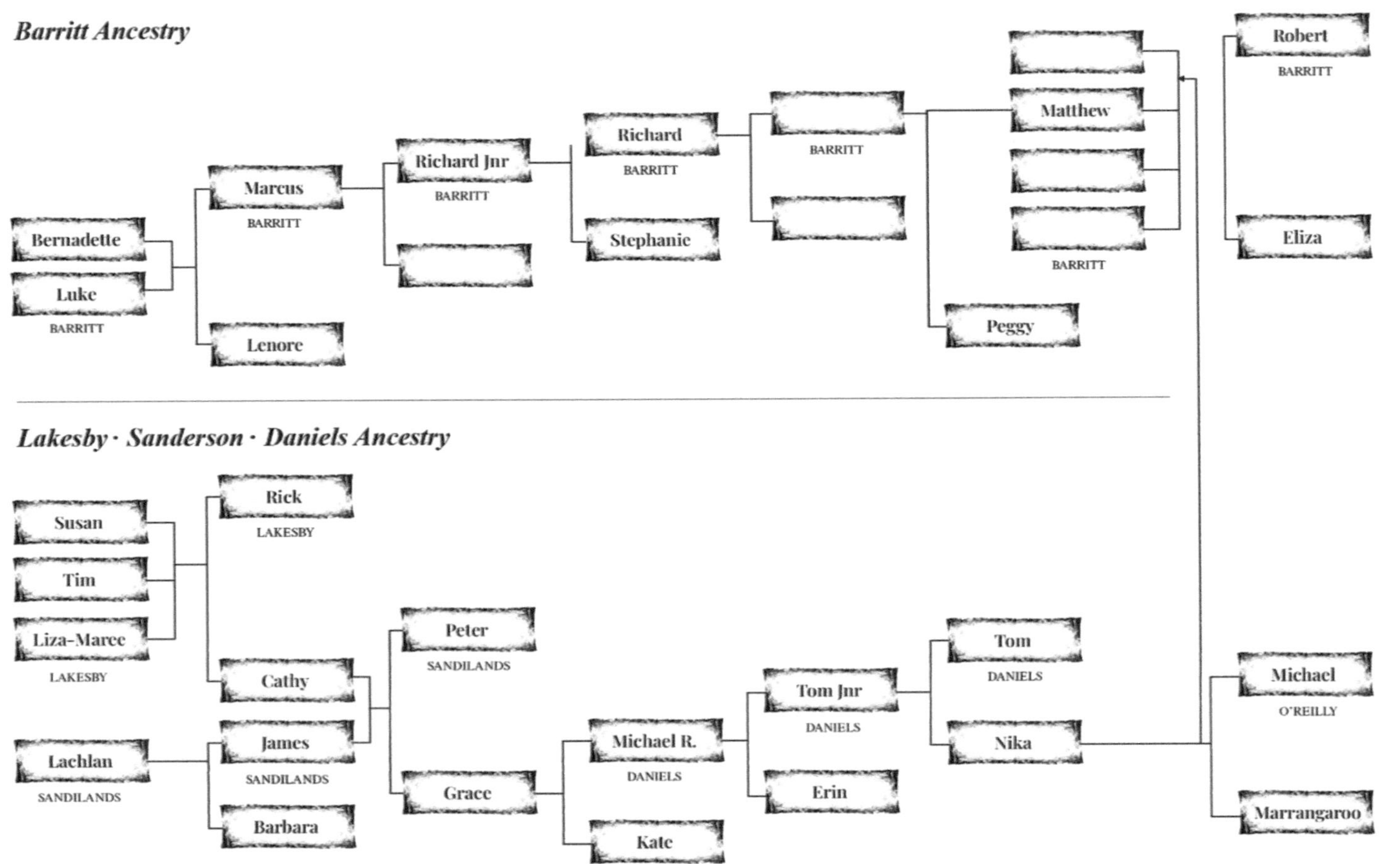

Barritt Ancestry
Bernadette
Luke
BARRITT
Marcus
BARRITT
Lenore
Richard Jnr
BARRITT
Richard
BARRITT
Stephanie
BARRITT
Matthew
BARRITT
Peggy
Robert
BARRITT
Eliza
Lakesby · Sanderson · Daniels Ancestry
Susan
Tim
Liza-Maree
LAKESBY
Rick
LAKESBY
Cathy
James
SANDILANDS
Barbara
Lachlan
SANDILANDS
Peter
SANDILANDS
Grace
Michael R.
DANIELS
Kate
Tom Jnr
DANIELS
Erin
Tom
DANIELS
Nika
Michael
O'REILLY
Marrangaroo

C H A P T E R I

Echoes

A golden-haired child danced. Sunlight filtered through a stand of gum trees. Small specks of lights played in the mane of her swinging hair.

The high point of her grandparents' thirty-three-acre property was a flat, rock-strewn area no larger than their lounge room. She carefully danced, and although sneakers are not appropriate footwear for dancing, they certainly protected her from possible sliding in any loose stones.

Max, the border collie dog, swirled and cavorted around the girl. Black and white with an almost white face, the patch of black over one eye emphasised his black ears with their little strands of white hair on the tips.

'Oh, Max! Max! What a beautiful day! I love it here!' She turned her face and lifted her arms towards the sun and continued her exuberant stepping and twirling.

When she slowed and then finally stopped, she knelt beside the animal. She hugged him and buried her face in his soft coat. He

1

barked, and this sound and her responsive ripple of laughter caught on the wind and whistled through the trees.

Her eyes focused for a moment on a bright spot near a tree root.

She moved to investigate. Her fingers scratched at the grass.

'It's only a stone.' She held it more closely to the sunlight. It was the purest white. For a moment, something of its natural beauty touched a chord in her heart. She placed it carefully in the pocket of her blue shorts and straightened the edge of her blue-and-white-striped sun top.

On a clear day from this high point, it was possible to see the white sand on a section of the distant shoreline and imagine the vast expanse of ocean beyond.

Someone, a long time ago, had made a rough wooden seat by carving out a section of a tree stump. It was still surprisingly comfortable.

Lisa sat. With the dog beside her, she rested and breathed in the peace and warmth of the summer day.

She felt Max quiver violently under her hand before she heard anything. He even softly whined. Then it came clearly – *a piercing crying sound.*

Heartbreakingly intense, it rose and fell on the wind. It was a cry of human grief, but there was also longing and a drawn-out sigh – almost like a question.

Why, Oh why, oh why? Lisa heard it in her ears but felt it more as pain in her heart. The sound ceased, but the vibration eerily resonated within.

She watched birds circling in the sky overhead and heard a kookaburra laugh to warn them of his territorial rights. She took another deep breath.

'Time we headed back, Max.'

The girl and the dog began their slow and careful return to the house.

'Gran! Grandad!'

Peter looked up when he heard the excited cry. Through the window, he watched as twelve-year-old Lisa Maree carefully ran now, down the final section of the rough, uneven path from the high point to the house. Max loped beside her or pranced in excited protective circles.

Peter marvelled at the grace and beauty of this, his youngest grandchild. No one else in the family had such beautiful golden hair.

She burst into the house and presented him with a small pure white rock.

'Look what I found,' she said excitedly. 'It's the colour of Max's forehead.' She laughed as the collie pushed into her and licked her hand. The mention of his name was enough to evoke his feelings of family partnership. Now maybe he'd also get some food. 'Sit, Max!' Peter held the stone in his hand. 'It *is* lovely.'

'Limga' Grace spoke softly behind him. 'Not sure when I first heard that, but my dad told me once that the Aboriginal word for any solid rock which had eternal properties was 'Limga'. It certainly is a beautiful specimen.'

She smiled. 'Let's have a cuppa. Sadly, Lisa will be leaving soon. Your mum phoned, love, she's coming to pick you up before lunch. She said your dad managed to get a campsite right near the beach at Inskip Point.

'Cathy sends love, by the way.' Grace smiled at Peter as they sat round a table which was already set with small plates of food and cups. 'She's always in a rush but sounded happy.'

Lisa quietly sipped her drink and nibbled a biscuit. She was pre-occupied. When she spoke, her words were cautious and edged with concern.

'Gran, do you know who cries at the high point of this property?' Grace gasped. 'Darling, whatever do you mean?'

'I he-heard a strange sound of crying as the wind blew through the trees. It was clear and very sad.' Her voice faltered. She sobbed.

Grace moved and warmly embraced the girl. She held her close. 'I lived here with my dad for a few years. We camped and lived in a small hut where the dam is now. Certainly, I never heard anything like that. I visited the high point many times over the years. It has always been peaceful and beautiful. It's only the wind, darling. It is stronger on the ridge today.'

Lisa was totally unconvinced. Sadness was real in her mind, and her heart had been irrevocably stirred. She swallowed, nodded, then returned their affectionate concern with a dazzling smile.

'Let's finish morning tea and perhaps play scrabble until your mum comes.'

'Let's play the board game at the table,' Peter quickly added, 'not on any devices.'

Lisa laughed. 'Oh, Poppy, you speak as if my iPad is an alien or something.'

Cathy's visit was brief. 'I'm sorry, guys, but I promised Rick we'd be in camp in time for lunch.' She embraced her parents warmly. 'Love you! Hop in the car now, darling,' she called urgently to Lisa.

Grace and Peter watched the four-wheel drive carefully travel down the hill to the entrance. Cathy and Lisa waved. 'Bye, Gran and Grandad. Thank you for two great days. We'll all be here for Christmas Day,' Lisa yelled.

Peter and Grace walked back to the house.

At the door, Grace abruptly stopped. Her face blanched.

'Oh, Pete! I've just remembered something.' She grabbed his arm. 'I'd forgotten all about it. One afternoon when we were living here – I was about ten – Dad came back from the high point looking very worried.

'"Grace, I heard someone crying," he said. "Do you think my mother was more upset about the bushfire burning down the old hut than she told us?"'

'Peter, my memories of Gran at that time were that she was sad about the loss of the hut but also happy to live in Gympie, near her friends. I wonder what Dad heard. I know it affected him very much.'

Peter sighed. 'Questions. We seem to be finding questions about stuff we have never worried about before. All triggered by Lisa today.' He gathered her in his arms and kissed the top of her head. 'Come on, dear, let's go for a walk.'

He whistled for Max who bounded towards them. They were grateful he stopped in time. His speed and enthusiasm could have knocked them over.

Later, on their return to the house, they concentrated on daily chores.

Max frolicked happily and for a time played with a ball. He even went off for a swim in the dam. It was a very hot, humid day.

'Oh, Max! You'll wet the floor.' Grace intercepted him at the door. For a short while, she played a ball game with him in the sunshine. When she sat on a chair in the veranda, he lovingly came and firmly placed a soggy, now muddy, paw in her lap. She groaned. His soulful brown eyes bored into her. 'Oh, you big sook, of course, you're not in trouble.' Bending down, she rubbed his chest. Water droplets fell as his body and tail furiously shuddered with appreciation and joy.

The phone rang.

Grace ran to answer it, and Max trotted behind. Light moisture showers followed in his wake.

'Hello, Grace speaking.'

'Gran, would you please remind Pop to turn on his mobile. I want to send him a text message as I'm currently travelling. I have a question to ask.'

Grace was pleased to hear from her grandson. Seventeen-year-old Lachlan stood more than six feet tall and, in both build and personality, was like a mirror image of their son James. *Perhaps that's why they don't get on very well. They are too alike.*

'I love my job, Gran, but will be interstate for the next two months.

I'll catch up with you and Pop in the New Year.'

Saddened he would not be with them for Christmas, she was still naturally curious about his question.

Peter muttered when she passed on the message. He'd reluctantly agreed to 'switch on his mobile' when he'd finished the mowing.

Lachlan's text did indeed raise another interesting family

question.

Do you have info re family who may have been lost in WW1? I have been selected to go with a youth group in 2015 to Anzac Cove and Villers-Bretonneux, possibly Fromelles in France. Some reported missing may be found.

Tks Pop lol Lockie

Peter's reply, like all his text messages, was brief.

No specific info but look for family names Sandilands and Daniels. See yuh Pop.

Echoes of the past were resonating.

Before this day was over, things from the past began to surface and clarify. It was as if bits of a large puzzle were falling into place.

First, it was the huge Christmas card attached to the Christmas tree. Called the Emily Card, it had been part of their Christmas décor for many years. It was a mountain scene decorated like an embossed painting.

Peter, who had seen it there for many years, always accepted it as being beautiful; he suddenly said, 'Grace, tell me again about Emily. What is her story?'

'Pete, I visited her once in 1965 in England only a few weeks before we met and married. She sadly died in 1966. She was apparently my father's grandmother's friend. She was an old lady when we met, but a grand lady, and I instantly warmed to her. I left feeling she was family. I loved her!

'She gave me a story she had written to bring home. It is about my mum and dad. I'll read it to you again, if you like, before Christmas. It's called "The Happiest Christmas of My Life".'

Thoughts of Emily were very real that night, and questions continued to be asked. Who was Emily Rickards?

What is her story?

CHAPTER II

Great-Aunt Emily Rickards

India

The birth of most babies is welcomed with joy. A few are unplanned, even unexpected. Some are unwanted.

At the crowded Bombay Marine Hospital, in its Maternity Wing called 'Hawa Mahal' (the name meant *constant sea breezes*), Emily Jane Rickards arrived at 11pm on 15 January 1869. A 7 lbs 5 oz bundle of wrinkled humanity, she screamed annoyance at this disruption to her previously quiet existence.

Her arrival at 'best' was… *inconvenient.*

Sergeant Ian McDonnell Rickards gazed down at his pretty Indian wife, Rani, with the child cradled in her arms. He sighed deeply.

He gently touched her hand then stooped and kissed her perspiring forehead.

He marched from the room and saluted the soldier who waited at the hospital entrance, and together they returned to the barracks of the Twenty-third Foot First Battalion, Bombay.

'An unfortunate liaison with the locals,' his friend Kirk muttered to him later in the Mess. 'Still you've got yourself a pretty little wife there, so I guess you'll have to make the best of it, old chap.' The chorus of voices in the barracks agreed, the glasses clinked, and beer flowed freely.

The early part of Emily's childhood was spent in British Army facilities where a procession of ayahs cared for her physical needs. Rani was an ever-present loving figure while her father remained as a background image who rarely came closer than a brief 'Hi there, kid!'

Journeying to Victorian England came in 1874. 'It's the safest place for her to be. So many children are dying here,' Ian said to a tearful Rani as they watched the liner depart from the harbour. 'We'll be returning to England very soon too, I expect. I trust Mrs Ferguson to deliver her safely to my mother's house in Bladon.'

They watched the tiny hand flutter its 'goodbye' as the small child, in a green jacket with matching hat, stood on tiptoes to catch a final glimpse of Mother and Father on the dock.

Martha Rickards felt the Victorian stoic approach was the best way of handling her deep grief at the news of the deaths of her son and daughter-in-law, still in India, from fever in 1878.

She simply stated to Emily, 'Well, child, your father's unwise Indian decisions mean it's you and me now. I guess we'll just have to make the best of it.'

Several years later, Emily was surprised by the interest in her story shown by a few of her work colleagues. Taking a rare break from the pressures of the day, they gathered round the heavy mahogany table in the workroom of the Berkley Bank in Fulham, London.

The men in their white starched winged-collared business suits lounged in the dark chairs with their polished armrests. They were interested but expressionless.

Accountant Derek Henderson leaned forward and watched the passion in her dark eyes, fascinated by her story and the tightly coiled bun of black hair as it bobbed when she nodded or emphasised a point.

'She never meant to be unkind,' Emily said.

'I never lacked anything. I had beautiful clothes and always adequate food and the best of education and comforts. In my heart, I knew she loved me, but never once did she ever tell me. When she died in 1900, I discovered I was her sole heir. I had inherited not only the Cotswold Cottage and land at Bladon but quite a bit of money as well! Because of the death in the Boer War of my dearest friend and fiancé William – my darling Will.' She paused in her story and swallowed as tears slid down her cheeks. 'He loved me, and for the first time in my life, I had felt with him something positive for the future.

'At the beginning of this new century, material possessions meant nothing to me at all, and I was overwhelmed by the emptiness and hopelessness of life.'

Derek shuffled in his chair and made a move to touch her hand, but she gently shook her head.

'One day I went to the library, and quite by accident, I read a story written by a young woman about the same age as myself. It was an article in the *Times* copied from the *Bulletin* in Australia. The writer lived in a faraway place called Gympie, apparently a mining town. The article was headed "Honouring My Mother's People and My Heritage". Her story of a mother from the first-nation people in Australia reminded me of my own mother who was from India.

'I decided to try and find her, so I sent a letter to the paper. She wrote back, and from that point, we have expanded our friendship. In our common sharing, I have found a friend but even more.

'Her husband is a Christian evangelist, and some of the things she shared about her life of faith, and their adventures in that small place have inspired many people. In a strange way, they have significantly helped me as well.

'I rented out the Cotswold Cottage in Bladon and came to London to work. I sent money to Nika to help with her charity work and more to help finance the hospital and home for displaced children she has established.

'Everything has a new sense of purpose, and they have "adopted" me as a kind of aunt. It is a lovely feeling to feel I now have a family in Australia. I am friend to Nika and Tom with the possibility of being Aunt Emily to any future children.' She laughed. 'They have encouraged me to seek and find a spiritual home and a church family here where I now live in a boarding house.

'Oh, I really must get back to work and concentrate. I wouldn't want to lose this job. I'm happy here.'

She left the table and walked back to her highly polished and engraved desk in the corner. The large cash book was still open, ready for her to continue entering precise and detailed figures in her neat handwriting.

Her high-necked white collar with matching cuffs on the sleeves contrasted to the deep green of the floor-length simple plain dress she wore. She walked carefully and sedately, but there was something of great dignity and beauty in her carriage.

A couple of the younger men swallowed, and Derek noticed young Sam blushed to the roots of his carroty red hair.

Only passage of time will reveal exactly what place Aunt Emily is destined to fulfil in the saga of the Daniels family.

CHAPTER III

The Happiest Christmas of My Life

Hillrock, Gympie 23 December 2014

Grace and Peter Daniels, in their comfortable chairs, sat in the lounge room.

'I love this time of year.' Grace smiled at the dancing lights on their Christmas tree. They reflected on the glass of the fish tank.

'Even the gold fish add their splash of colour,' Peter commented.

Max ambled in and plopped down between their chairs. He carefully assessed both human faces with his soft brown eyes, rearranged his blanket, and then assumed his guarding position of perfect peace.

'No snoring now, mate. Let this night keep its peace.'

Outside the inky darkness was pierced by a canopy of stars stretching across the sky above the trees. There was no breeze, but the stillness had a breathless hush of expectancy. The cooling of the ground after the searing heat of a summer day rose in tiny spirals of mist from rocks and grassless areas. All life waited for rain to restore and replenish.

'Please let's keep the telly off for a while,' Peter said. 'When we were first married, you shared Emily's story. Somehow, this Christmas is different – the past, the present, and the future (now we are getting older) seem to be raising questions and seeking answers.'

Grace opened the folder and removed the pages held together by a brown clip.

She read with feelings:

1941. Bladon, Oxfordshire. England

The Happiest Christmas of My Life

How strange! In the midst of a dreadful war with stories of bombings, death, and dying, I record this Christmas as the happiest of my life. It was not about 'externals'; it was all about 'internals' this year. Ties that bind. Love and family not always of the same blood but intrinsically connected by heart values and faith. This defies human logic but challenges attitude to everything.

I heard the doorbell ring. It was 2.30pm on a bitterly cold Christmas Eve afternoon in 1941. My heart pounded furiously. I opened the door.

He stood there. Tall, sandy-haired, smiling (just as I imagined). His khaki military uniform looked Australian and his slouch hat had the jaunty almost cheerful tilt I expected from Aussie soldiers. There was an additional Union Jack insignia on his pocket. He told me later this was because of his civilian job in London with cypher codes, and his desire to remain and serve in England.

Kate was as lovely as I expected. Her long dark hair complemented stunningly her cherry-red coat and black boots. Their five-month-old baby daughter was asleep and wrapped parcel-like, and supported between them.

I ran to greet them. Quite spontaneously I found myself enveloped by embraces of incredible warmth and 'connection'.

This was Michael – my dear friend's grandson – his family and I felt for the first time in my life like I belonged. In some strange indefinable way, it was a God Gift.

William, the love of my life, did not return from the Boer War but here now – a Gift – a young soldier and his family. My sense of belonging. Not distant by letter and heart but physically here. There was no British restraint from me – I can't explain it. We all stood. Tears flowed. Healing for past 'losses' came but incredible gratitude for the present washed over us like a river.

Michael had to return to duty in London on Boxing Day but we had this afternoon, this night, the next day and night. Christmas was 'ours'. We would live it as an oasis in a world gone mad with trouble and strife.

This slate-roofed Cotswold Cottage bequeathed to me by my grandmother would, in my lifetime, become a beautiful modern home. In 1941 it was more simple but Christmas transformed the atmosphere. The decorations were sparse but beautiful angels and stars decorated fir tree branches and there was a lingering smell of earth and woodland.

I could record in this story about food. Yes, beautiful food. Rationing was in place but what we had was adequate and sustaining.

Michael and Kate looked happy. Grace was a smiling, contented, strong-willed baby who liked attention but had the ability to become totally absorbed by colour and light. It was a joy to hear her chuckle.

Christmas Eve we walked to St Martin's Church. It was extremely cold but the village cottages clustered around the church and it was a very short walk.

Thank God for it ALL. The church bells seemed to ring

out a defiant Hope for a better future. This special Child we celebrate brought with Him the PEACE which defies understanding. In the middle of chaos and heartache His Peace is the internal kind. Beyond understanding. We stood outside for a moment and simply held each other.

Inside was the warmth of community. Comfort found for grief as war and losses still ravaged lives but yet... yet hard to write here but in this Christmas, Christ Who Is Christmas met each one of us. The sermon was inspiring and inspirational. No need to explain for Kate and Michael knew as I did the powerful Presence of God in the place but also in us individually and knew He would carry us into the future.

Yes, we were happy – almost deliriously so. We were aware of need for lights to be extinguished and for blackout curtains. Even on this night certain places in the world were bombed and people died but here, here, for one memorable Christmas I knew God was with us. Hope for a future was strong. We laughed, we played word games in the gloom. We cried and danced and made fools of ourselves in funny hats.

Thank You Lord for fulfilling in 1941 your Promises to me that one day my friend from across the world would 'connect' with me.

Michael, Kate, and baby Grace. Thank you for 'being' family. Thank you too for the Happiest Christmas of My Life.

Emily Rickards.

Grace carefully clipped the pages and placed the story back in a folder.

'I wish I could have known her,' Peter commented.

'When I met her in 1965, she lived in Bladon in a beautiful two-storied home. She was ninety-six years old, still active and strong. How I wish now I could have stayed longer than one day. Perhaps she could have helped me unravel some of the mysteries of what

14

happened next?

'My dad was restrained from talking by the Official "Secrets" Act. Only in more recent times I've been told we can investigate and find some truths.'

'Sometimes, the past is safer in the past as we pray only the 'good' will come to the surface.' Peter smiled. 'Would you like a sherry, love? We've got peanuts and some popcorn that won't deplete the Christmas stores. Then maybe the *Andre Rieu Christmas Special* will have something meaningful and less razz and jangle and ho! ho! ho! than some of the other stuff.'

Grace laughed. 'Yes, please. Christmas is coming. Let's hope we can be ourselves, show *love* to our folks, and not become "stressed" by attitudes.'

* * * Their evening was gentle and peaceful.

Although sleep is a necessary part of living, sometimes, thoughts and memories swirl in the darkness, and only waking produces any clarity.

The screaming drawn-out wail of an air-raid siren sounded. A silence was followed by a profound eerie breathless hush – then something happened – a scream – followed by more and more screams. People were dead, and their bodies were laid in neat little rows. Even small children lay side by side.

A man's desperate voice cried out. 'NO!'

'Grace! Wake up!' She woke, shaking violently. She reached instinctively for Peter's hand. 'Oh, love, what's wrong?' He embraced her, tightly close, until the shaking subsided.

She was finally able to answer.

'I... I'm not sure. It was a dream but vivid and very real. Why now is what's so surprising. Once a long time ago my father told me my mum and baby brother died because of an air raid. I... t... think it was in London.

'I believe he prayed with me. He told me we prayed for them

together. He said then, "The past is best left in the past. Let the dead rest in peace." He had simply and gently answered my question about my mother.'

'Maybe he's right. It's what we have, and being contented, that's the most important thing. I'll put the jug on, and we'll have a cuppa and watch the sun come up.' He was cheerful and reassuring. 'Today we give thanks for this new day and for personal health and strength.'

She hugged him tightly. 'Questions. Questions. Questions. I'm sorry I didn't get more answers before Dad died. What was he doing overseas? Why, when we came home to Australia in 1943, did I have to stay with my gran while he went to work? He never came home much. It's all very vague in my mind. I only know it was in Gympie.

'Dad told me this property here just out of town was a legacy. A bushfire destroyed the small hut in 1939. We lived here for a few years, and I went to the little local school. I loved it. Peter, there are many unanswered questions. I should have asked him. I'm told by others that a lot of men after the war simply would not talk about it. Guess I'll only find answers now if I do research.' She laughed. 'Perhaps I'll do a Google search. So much for modern technology.'

'Ah, I don't think you'll gain anything by digging up the past.'

'I know you're right, love, but I find suddenly and unexpectedly I really would like to know.'

Her nightmare was the edge of the story. Records one day will reveal the whole legacy.

CHAPTER IV

Michael Robert Daniels

(Grace's Father) Born 1915

London 1943

3 March. The air-raid siren sounded at 8.17pm. Everyone was on high alert because of the acceleration of the war and the bombing of Berlin on 1 March.

Michael Daniels, Kate, and the two children would not have been on the street except for the spontaneous decision to take the baby for a short walk to 'settle' him.

Michael held twenty-month-old Grace who snuggled into his shoulder and happily played with the shoulder lapels on his military uniform. Kate cradled three-day-old Trevor.

'I need to head back to barracks soon, love.' Michael squeezed Kate's shoulder and for a moment touched the fall of her long black hair. 'I'll see you and the children safely settled back at the boarding house and then head off. Emily is looking forward to your spending the rest of the war safely in the country with her. We'll go there at the weekend.'

'Michael, I hate us to be separated. It was wonderful to have you present at Trevor's birth. I'm happy to stay here near the barracks.'

The piercing wail of the siren drowned out his smiling response.

What happened next would never with certainty be known. It was sudden and unexpected and unfolded as one of the tragedies of the Second World War.

People moved in a surging mass towards the Bethnal Green Air-raid Shelter. This adequate large facility had steps leading down into a massive cavern below. For safety, there was lighting. Blackout requirements meant it was eerily dim. The crowd was disciplined and orderly, but someone on the steps slipped... fell, . . . crashed into the people in front who also fell. A section of the people following also lost their balance and tumbled into the opening. Someone screamed. Anxious people in the street, unmindful of the source of this terror, continued to surge forward. Somehow, Kate was swept along with this tide of frightened people as the siren continued to wail.

Michael lost sight of her and remembered little else but clutching Grace tightly to his chest as he toppled headlong into an alley with several people falling on top and beside him. Everything was inky blank, and he lost consciousness when his head hit the ground.

He came to with the sounds of human screaming pounding in his ears. The siren was silent. He learnt later that a bomb fell two streets from the shelter but did not detonate perhaps due to French Resistance sabotage.

He struggled to a sitting position and shuffled against a wall. His legs were now free. Grace struggled in his tightly locked arms. She smiled. Dust covered her face, and there was a spot of blood on her nose. 'We've felled, oder,' she commented tearfully.

Dazed people around them slowly moved and assessed their injuries.

The next morning Michael learned that along with many others, Kate and the baby had died in the crush.

Grief tore through his soul like a knife.

Apart from bruising and a few minor cuts, Michael and Grace were unhurt.

Medical staff forced them to remain in hospital until the doctors gave clearance. They arrived at the boarding house in the late afternoon.

Elsa McGregor met them at the door. 'Ooh,' she moaned. 'Me darlings, me poor darlings.' She embraced them with all the maternal warmth of her heart. Her ample breasts enfolded them. 'Oh, 'tis sorry I am. So very sorry.'

Grace went to bed quite happily with Elsa and only murmured, 'Mummy?' as she drifted off to sleep.

Elsa returned to sit beside Michael on the sofa. The blackout curtains shrouded the dimly lit room with an eerie glow. 'Hadn't you best be heading back to barracks, son?' she asked gently. 'You don't want the MPs arriving with an AWL order.'

'I don't care,' he sobbed. 'I simply don't care. They can do what they like. I'm not going anywhere until Kate and Trevor are buried. I hate this rotten war! I hate senseless cruelty and tragedies. I hate life and the unfair senselessness of it *all*.'

She sat beside him and held him as the violence of grief, anger, and pain rolled over him in waves.

Later, she made a cup of tea, and he finally fell into a deep and troubled sleep.

The morning brought a curt telegram from the barracks.

TRAGEDY KNOWN. RETURN TO DUTIES MARCH 8 0800 HOURS.

Colonel P. Wainwright.

Royal Artillery Barracks, Woolwich, Royal Borough of Greenwich, London.

8 March. The silver plate on the door read, 'Colonel P. Wainwright'.

Michael straightened his uniform. He felt sick – grief was a constricting band around his stomach. He knocked.

'COME IN!' barked an authoritative voice. 'Sit down, son,' he said more gently.

Michael saluted and sank into the chair indicated by the colonel's hand.

'First, soldier,' he spoke again with obvious sincerity, 'I'm sorry to hear of your tragic loss. If there is anything I can do, please let me know.'

'I would like to go home, sir. That's what I want now more than anything else.'

'With the war at its present stage, I think that is very unlikely. You are needed here. Your special training with the Signals Corps, particularly in the code- breaking and identification area, is highly valued. You are Australian, I believe. Exactly where is your home?

'I come from Gympie in Queensland, sir. You've probably not heard of the place.'

The colonel laughed. 'My knowledge of Australia, I'm afraid, is limited to Sydney and Melbourne. Wait here for a few minutes, son. Take a break, relax. There are a couple of Australian war files I would like to look through.'

When he returned to the office, he slammed a thick folder on his desk. 'I don't know why in this world of such tragedy, moments of surprise like this still occur.'

'Sergeant Michael Daniels, it's rather splendid that I find I am able to officially transfer you to Gympie, Queensland, Australia. Your job will have a classified certification and will be a worthwhile contribution to the war effort. Enhancing, I believe, protection for your own nation as well. If you can be ready in a few days, I will arrange passage on a troop carrier for you and Grace. This is most unusual. You will be amazed when you get home. I would say for those who believe in such things, the timing is nothing short of a miracle.'

'By God! A miracle indeed,' he added with a gruff laugh.

'Thank you, sir.' Michael stood, saluted, and marched from the colonel's office.

Surprise, added to the shock of the past few days, hit him suddenly. His legs trembled violently as he walked across the parade ground to the main office building. He fell into the chair at his desk. As he cradled his head in his cupped hands, he breathed gently and regularly. Shaking ceased eventually, and something stirred in his heart. It was a thin trickle of hope.

11 March

The mound of freshly dug earth within the grounds of St John's Parish Church, Bethnal Green, was washed by rain and glistened in the early morning light. Michael fell to his knees. Raw grief was paralyzing, and he was surprised by the desperate need to pray.

He reached out. His hand rested on the mound.

'Lord God. It's been a long time since I've prayed. The faith of my childhood and the legacy from grandparents somehow has become lost and unreal in my world of war and grief, yet these my beloved wife and child – I need to surrender them both into the Hands of Forgiveness and Grace of the One in whom I thought I had stopped believing.

'O God, if you are there, help me in this hour of need. Please keep my heart from thoughts of anger, hatred, or revenge. May my beloved rest in peace. Grant that my daughter and I may journey on tomorrow back to a life and purpose and a future. In Jesus' name, amen. All things unto YOU!'

Rain continued to fall. His heart ached unbearably, but something within shifted. A heavy weight became lighter. Peace inexplicably washed over him in supernatural waves. He fell prone to the ground and sobbed.

❦

20 March 1943

Dear Emily,

Security prevents me from giving much information here. I can only confirm with a broken heart the tragic deaths of Kate and our three-day-old son.

Grace and I are both unhurt and well. We are returning to Australia and through a set of circumstances – miraculous? We are going directly to Gympie. (My mother will be overjoyed.)

Gratitude always for your love. Regret inability to be with you last Christmas. You will always be in our hearts and we indeed value your prayers. I am personally still struggling.

Love, Michael

Gympie, April 1943

The puffing train rattled and rolled its way north from Brisbane on 30 April.

Coal fragments drifted through open windows. Michael picked out specks from his daughter's black curls and dusted them off her blue bonnet. She had been restless and fretful for most of the journey. 'Poor little one,' he murmured. *All the long sea voyage must have been hard for you. More for me than you, perhaps. All the fellows – soldiers and sailors constantly at hand to keep you entertained.* He laughed, as his thoughts ambled back to the good times and then stopped for a moment remembering the bad. *All those anxious nights when the ocean rolled, the vessel tossed, and we lived with the constant anxiety that the inky blackness could be hiding an*

22

'I'm grateful and thankful we are safely here, little one.' He kissed her cheek.

The train pulled into Gympie Station. A few military personnel disembarked from the very full train, but more soldiers in full battle fatigues boarded.

'Townsville,' one fresh-faced soldier commented to Michael as he passed.

The platform was a bustling throng of uniforms, conversation, and noise. American accents contrasted strongly with the mixture of state-by-state Australian.

Passengers heading south were mainly Americans whose postings to training areas in Brisbane annoyed the soldiers heading north to Townsville. They were being sent there for deployment to areas needing coastal protection. Some would go further north to join larger military operations.

One American taunt 'Don't worry about your girls – we'll take care of them' started a fight that only the arrival of the train heading south prevented from becoming an all-out brawl.

Amid the smoke, dust, and confusion, Michael's eyes scanned the platform.

His mother stood at the far end. She saw him. Her expression was hidden by the brim of her large white panama hat, and a slight breeze teased at the hem of her brightly patterned dress. He suspected she was crying.

Holding Grace firmly against his shoulder, he dragged a large kit bag behind him. He moved to greet her.

'Darling!' Erin's voice cracked with emotion. 'When the army contacted me to say you were being posted here to Gympie, I couldn't believe it. So many prayers, so much hope for your return one day. Now you're actually here. You are home!'

Unrestrained tears streamed down her face as she added, 'My heart breaks for you and the loss of Kate and Trevor. Thank God that you and Grace have made it here.'

In a rush of emotion, the kit bag was dropped as the three

huddled together. For a short time, the world around disappeared. 'I'm home but not on holidays,' Michael murmured. He struggled to reach her face under the large brim of her panama but hoped he kissed her cheek. 'Home but uncertain what my job will be.'

'Well, for a start I've been cautioned by the military not to advertise your return too widely. No welcome-home events or "loose" talk with neighbours.' She laughed.

'How am I going to explain the child when I walk down Mary Street? Even with an immaculate conception, she's too old to be mine.' She unexpectedly giggled. 'It would be kind of fun to pretend though.' Grace, now in her grandmother's arms, wriggled and began to cry.

'Here, Mum, I'll carry her till we get home.'

'Down. Daddy, down!' Grace suddenly bellowed. She threshed her arms and legs and struggled to her feet. She was unsteady, but with her gran and father's support, they all slowly left on the platform's exit ramp. Her dark curls bounced, and her blue bonnet slid to hang down her back on its ribbon as she determinedly walked onward.

'What's happened to all the beautiful flowers that used to grow in the garden beds along the platform?' Michael suddenly asked. 'It all looks so barren now!'

'Oh, darling, much has changed since the Japanese entered the war in 1941. We are on strict security alerts now, and the flowers which clearly spelt out the identification of the station were considered a security risk. Tuesday last week, we had a scare when a small seaplane flew over the Gympie area. It was obviously Japanese. It's clear, bright red sun markings, on fuselage and wings, shone in the sunlight. This was later confirmed by the air force. Planes were sent from Amberley to ensure that it had not lingered. I was out walking and witnessed the plane fly over, so I was told later by a soldier, they believed it was on a photographic mission.'

'Mum, I had no idea the war was close to you folks here. No idea at all.'

'A lot's been going on, love, but I guess you'll learn soon enough. We've got army people camping all along Old Maryborough Road and some sort of military set-up on the south side. Local folks are still milking cows and chasing after livestock in the middle of all this change. There was a story last week of a little boy with his dog who were trying to round up a wandering cow. She headed straight for the Mess Hut in the army camp and overturned a barrel of potatoes. Stories abound about the soldiers who tried to stop the rolling spuds from getting under tent flaps or into the horses' corral. They were great with the kid though. They caught the cow and helped him get her home.'

Slowly they continued their walk until Grace was tired enough to be carried, and they turned into the street above Mary Street, to Erin's home. Again, Michael noticed something unusual. The names of some of streets had been changed. 'Why is it no longer called Nash Street?' he asked puzzled. Erin laughed. 'Another security issue I believe. Some of the street names have been altered as a confusing device if someone was "spying". For public safety, we were told. They'll be changed back again when the war is over.'

He was astonished. 'So much has changed. So much!'

'Welcome home, darling. Welcome back to your grandparents' place. It seems difficult to believe they've been gone now eleven years.'

They stopped in front of the white pivot fence and looked at the simple but gently beautiful timber cottage that once belonged to Nika and Tom. The taped and blacked-out windows added a mysterious quality to its gentle charm.

'I'll make us all a cuppa, and then we can sit and have a good talk.

Mike, it's like a miracle that you are here again. Come in.'

Michael struggled to contain his emotions as he sat with Grace on his lap, in the large lounge, and looked around the home he had loved as a small child. He had not seen it for five years.

'That cup of tea will be appreciated. All of this is amazing to me as well. I'm sure in the morning I'll wake up and find everything in the past few weeks has been a nightmare/dream and I'm still in England.'

He hugged Grace more tightly against his chest and sighed deeply. The smile he directed to his mother was warm and, although sad, had the sparkle of hopefulness and confidence she remembered well.

1944

'Life has changed dramatically since Michael came home,' Erin Daniels remarked to the small group of mothers gathered on the floor of the Nash Street home's new extension porch. 'We rarely see him, have no idea what he is doing, but the war is far away for Grace and me. Our days are filled with explorations and new adventures. I realise now the great joy grandchildren bring.'

Worldwide, the war still raged, and the small Gympie community once again displayed its huge 'heart' throbbing with hope for a better tomorrow.

All churches furiously worked with ladies' groups and men's carving work sheds (specially designed for toy making). Red Cross, CWA, Rotary, Lions, Apex. More help organisations contributed to collective aid parcels than were listed. Motivation to help kept small community organisations constantly busy. The 'collective' contributions per capita stood among the highest in the land.

Yet, out in the wider world, suffering and dying continued throughout the five opening years of the 1940s. A new generation of widows and fatherless children walked Gympie streets waiting for news of soldiers overseas. Often anxious eyes scanned the skies wondering if enemy planes would come and they too would be in the thick of conflict.

Older people and women and children stoically determined to keep farms and properties alive.

'Life for us really is good,' Erin continued. 'We're fortunate there are movies, plays, books to read, regular bush dances, and many fun activities for children. Hope is high for an end to this war and for a community that will expand and continue to grow. This thought is strong in every heart.'

One young mother commented quietly, 'I feel guilty some days I am so busy, I don't have time to think of anything else but "keeping the home fires burning".' She laughed. 'I can certainly understand how your life has changed, Erin.'

'Grace is certainly the "miracle" addition to my life.'

Hearing her name, the girl with the tangle of dark curls, dressed in a blue frilly pinafore, and sturdy brown shoes, suddenly stood up. Smiling expansively, she cried out, 'Nana!' The circle of tightly grouped children was momentarily destabilised. One boy fell over, and his block creation tumbled to the floor with a thud.

A coloured block then mysteriously became airborne and hit Grace on the arm. She sat down wailing, more from annoyance than pain. Small bodies hurtled from all directions. 'He hurt Grace!' Tommy Cosgrove yelled as he shoved blond Timmy James's shoulder. Timmy fell on top of Grace, and they both started crying. Two small girls flung themselves into the melee. They too started crying for no obvious reason. Mothers and grandmothers separated, soothed, consoled, and chastised offspring.

'I think it's time we took them home for a sleep,' Mavis Cosgrove said as she clasped Tommy's hand, gathered up an extraordinary amount of personal paraphernalia, and prepared to leave. 'Bye, everyone. Thank you, Erin, for a lovely morning. My place, next week, 10am. Bye, all!'

They all lived locally, and walking home in the sunshine added to the morning outing. For many of these young women, news from loved ones, fighting overseas, remained limited. Sometimes it was weeks, even months between letters.

21 July 1944

The tall soldier, in khaki uniform and slouch-hatted, halted for a moment. He watched the children gather around a picnic cloth on parkland beside the Mary River. It was Grace's third birthday, and seven little ones and their parents had joined her for cake and fruit slices to celebrate. He smiled, but Grace had sighted him and already was running across the park. 'Daddy!' she screamed, and lots of little ones ran after her all calling, 'It's a daddy!' Michael stopped, stooped, then warmly hugged his daughter. Little arms swamped him, and happy children's laughter rang through the treetops. Like the Pied Piper, he slowly walked towards the adults.

'I'm glad you could get time off,' Erin said as she kissed him. He dropped beside her on the rug.

The winter chill had today been warmed by noonday sun. The rising pile of cardigans and jackets, near the food baskets, testified to the temperature. Michael fervently wished he too could get some of the gear 'off'. Instead, he stretched and smiled at his mother.

'The war is not going well,' he quietly whispered. 'I don't think it'll be over by Christmas as we all thought. Death tolls are rising in all countries, and right now the Pacific conflict is at its most vicious. Oh, Mum.' Suddenly his voice broke, and Erin embraced him tightly. 'Sometimes, I wish I could be fighting "out there" with the army. Actively involved! Being told that my job is vitally important doesn't stop the heartache sometimes. Did my dad die for nothing?

'Are my wife and son destined to be no more than memories in an ocean of lives cut short, with potentials never reached?' Erin held him and allowed the unexpected flow of his tears to fall. 'It's listening to the heavily censored reports and knowing the true picture is much worse that I find the hardest.'

Grace looked up from the game they were playing and saw her nan and dad embracing. She ran with outstretched arms and joined them in a massive hug. 'I love you,' she called. 'An, and... today I'm three, that's... one, two, and three.' She counted on her fingers and laughed happily. 'I'm a big girl now!'

'She's the reason, my love, why we have hope. When your father disappeared, it was you who gave me the reason to believe for a future.'

She gathered Grace onto her lap, and the three hugged tightly. 'One day, one day, the mystery of lost people will be solved. Bodies will be found, and above all eternal certainties of our human purposes on this earth will be discovered. One day.'

CHAPTER V

Letter from Gympie

1960

Dear Emily,

Your last letter made me conscious of the big gaps in our lives in which you have expressed an interest.

I'll try to fill in some of the 'bits' you asked about.

Yes indeed, the 1946 celebrations of peace were incredible. Not as big as yours in London but with the Light Horse, military bands, all the precision and dignity plus the overwhelming relief of ordinary people. It was a great occasion.

Yet, truth to tell, after the war, I 'dropped out' for many years. I settled back into Hillrock with Grace. My mum Erin returned to stay in town after living with us for a couple of years. She loved the Nash Street house and had many friends and a great social life.

We grew our own vegetables but lack of rain and summer heat made our fruit growing less productive. We do however still have two mango trees, a struggling loquat tree, and a small patch of bananas near the dam. I looked after Hillrock and worked on nearby properties to supplement income.

Grace and I lived quietly and very simply. We wanted for nothing and somehow the years passed. Our letters to you in this period were indeed sparse but we were happy and no, dear, there was nothing you could have done to improve our lives.

I'm delighted to hear of your wonderful cruises to the Greek Islands and – my goodness – six months in Spain. Well done! Hope you have returned to 100% health now.

Big news, this end is still being digested. My sixty-three-year-old mum is to be married in June. She is marrying Patrick O'Laughlin, an Irish bowling friend for the past four years. They are moving to Ireland for an indefinite period. Patrick is a great chap, only three years her senior. I pray their lives will be blessed by God and they will travel comfortably and well. For Erin, she hopes she'll find relatives who may remember her parents who immigrated seventy years ago.

This letter is written from Nash Street. We moved back here when Grace went to high school. Hillrock is visited and maintained regularly. The small hut near the dam remains a sanctuary and an often weekend retreat.

Grace loves her job with the firm of solicitors in the Mary Street Office. She is including in this letter her story. 'Grace's Journey' she wrote in her diary. She thought you may be interested.

Stay well and be happy. Some days I long to come back to England to visit but perhaps it will be Grace who sees you first.

Lots of love and thank you for caring.

'My Journey'

From child to young woman – by Grace Daniels

Memories are powerful reminders of past events. My early journey is recorded as a simple narrative here. Maybe it will fill in gaps if anyone is researching in the future and wonders about our life.

The 1946 Victory Celebrations are remembered as lots of noise and excitement. Gran cried, and Dad, still wearing his uniform, had a funny happy/sad expression on his face.

My father always insisted the Official Secrets Act prevented him from telling me about his wartime job in Gympie. I never asked questions, but when we moved to Hillrock, he was often very quiet and spent a lot of days writing. He compiled notes and records which he stored in a box in the little office annex he built adjoining the hut.

'Memories,' Gran once commented to me. 'He has lots of memories of life before you were born and wants to keep them stored in written form.'

Our life was quiet and interesting. Dad built the new hut on the foundations of the old, from natural resources. Gran spent many happy hours making the inside 'homely'.

She returned to live in Gympie when I started school. We missed her, but Dad and I had a great life together. I had a small dog named Peg, and together we walked the property, exploring.

Our two horses were agisted in a neighbour's bottom paddock as his grass was better for horses than ours. Our cow Bessie thrived in her paddock with its shelter and milking hut at the far end.

Dad was always busy. From early morning until dusk, he was working somewhere. He looked after our own place but supplemented income from regular jobs he had on nearby properties.

Grace added in her own handwriting an addition to her father's letter.

Dear Emily,

I'm not sure if you are interested in all of this but you did say 'fill in the gaps'. I kept my Year 7 composition called 'Going to School... I Remember...'

Going to School... I Remember . . .

I started school in February 1947, and my first day is very clear. We left home after Bessie was milked. Peg wanted to come so had to be tied up. She howled plaintively as we galloped away. I was on horseback in front of Dad. He shouted, 'Don't worry, dog, I'll be back soon.'

The sign outside the small timber building read Wolvi State School. Dad explained 'Wolvi' means a young kangaroo. Bigger than a 'joey' but still young enough to get in the mother's pouch if there is room.

Miss Jane Jenkins met me at the door. She looked huge, but in hindsight, I guess she was average in height and build. It was me who was so small.

'Hello, Grace. Welcome!' Her hair was in a knob, and her cheerful face trembled in the benevolence of her wide smile.

Dad kissed my cheek and whistled to Dancer, his black stallion, who stood patiently in the fenced enclosure with other horses. One little white Austin car was proudly parked in an adjoining area.

Dancer neighed an excited welcome to his master. I remember how proudly my dad rode away, not looking back, but giving me a confident wave. 'I'll be back at three thirty. Enjoy your day.'

I took Miss Jenkins's hand. I remember my own hand trembled. We disappeared inside. I felt my life of 'freedom' was over, and nothing would ever be the same. I struggled not to cry but felt hot tears sliding down my cheeks.

1947–1953

These years are my happily remembered school years. I loved the little school. I loved the teachers. I later believed no child in any place or any community could have had a better general education. As a child with no mother, it was a nurturing place. I received more than just learning at that little school. It was family.

'Your eyes are shining,' Dad remarked one day.

'Oh yes, today we had a play. It was all about a king called Arthur. I was the one who burnt his cakes.' Dad laughed. He was always interested in my school life and family.

We returned to live in Gympie and I gained entrance to Gympie High School in 1954. One teacher there remembered Dad who attended 1928–1933.

Now, Emily, here we are in 1960. I've gone from child to young woman. I wonder what the years ahead will bring. Gran is going to Ireland. Dad often lives now for periods of time at Hillrock, and I stay in town close to my job. I have assured him I will be fine when Gran goes to Ireland. Both Gran and Dad encourage me to save and travel overseas one day. Perhaps I'll do this in the future but leaving Dad will be very hard.

Much love from me.

Grace

CHAPTER VI

Christmas Day 2014

Hillrock, Gympie

A hot, humid Christmas morning gradually mellowed as the afternoon breeze stirred gum trees and cooled the wide, airy veranda of the house.

Inside, the Christmas tree sparkled with lights and tinsel. The cleared table with its bright red tablecloth still showed the festive disarray of broken Christmas crackers, party hats, and crumbs from lunch's happy chaos.

Peter reclined in his favourite chair. Before him was again played out the usual activities that swirled when the season brought the family together. He smiled.

We love them all so much. We will never be able to give them faith or the lessons the Spirit has taught us through the years. We can only pray that love *and example will help point them to meaningful life paths.*

Grace sat with Lisa. Grey head and golden one were close as they concentrated on the game of stacking tiny chairs. One red one suddenly caught by a gust of wind, tumbled, spiralled, and rolled across the lawn.

Max was after it. Like a streak of black-and-white lightning, he bounded across the yard. He caught it. Holding it in his teeth, he proudly pranced back to Lisa. He dropped it on her foot and sat grinning his doggy smile. Enthusiasm vibrated his whole body. Even accidental games made his day! The family was almost complete. Cathy and husband Rick had come with Lisa and their older children Susan and Tim. James and his wife, their daughter-in-law Barbara, were quiet and had an air of sadness about them. It was Lachlan's first Christmas away. Peter knew they missed their seventeen-year-old son as much as he missed his vivacious and funny eldest grandchild.

While they played an enthusiastic version of their own game of softball, sixteen-year-old Susan also looked particularly unhappy.

I'll speak with her later if I get the opportunity, Peter thought. 'Would anyone like a cool drink or something more to eat?'

'No more food. Thanks, Dad,' Cathy answered. This was echoed by several confirming voices.

'Coffee please, love,' Grace replied.

He went inside and placed glasses, cold water, fruit juice, sherry, a couple of beers, and a prepared coffee on a tray.

He noticed the Christmas tree drooped in the heat. It wasn't a real tree, but summer temperatures made the baubles and streamers appear heavier. Even the angel on top was askew and her wings decidedly off-centre now.

At least Cathy and James are speaking to each other. I hate it when our children are not getting on. They've very different temperaments, our daughter and son.

His thoughts continued to ramble. *Looking at them you can clearly see the secular influences on their lives. It's not just the fun things like the Santa hats and the flashing earrings and T-shirts but a tension — false joy — a kind of desperate attempt to be 'happy'. Grandson Lachlan is the only one who has clear life goals and has a heart with Christian intent. It's a shame he decided to stay away rather than be with his father. Why oh why are James and Barbara so against his wanting to work in Thailand?*

'Hi, Pop. I'll take this tray out for you. Everyone can help themselves. I'll give Gran her coffee.' Susan gave him one of her radiant smiles and tossed her head. Her Christmas earrings jangled furiously.

'Thanks, love. When you've left them on the table, grab a drink for yourself. Then come back and talk with me for a bit.'

She didn't come straight back, but a short time later he looked up. She was beside him. 'Pop,' she said hesitantly, 'I really would like to talk.'

Her words then came in a rush. 'Pop, there's this boy I like. His name is Tanuka. He comes from Vanuatu. He's in the same media class as me at college. He's a fantastic person, but Mum and Dad seem worried I'll get too fond of him. Why are they concerned and frightened I might go and live away somewhere? It's not as if they'll miss me. They're both so busy I hardly see them. Most times at home now, I feel like I'm invisible.'

Cathy and Rick, both talented, gifted people, driven by your own career goals. Slow down, please, slow down. Peter's thoughts raced. He put his arm around Susan. She rested her head on his shoulder. 'I don't have answers, love, but I would like to pray with you, and for you.'

She hesitated but, drawn by his love and concern, nodded.

Gracious Father, draw Susan by your Grace into an awareness of You. May she then be able to clearly make wise and clear decisions in her life. In Jesus' name, amen.

The heat of the summer's day slowly lessened as breezes from the distant ocean and incoming tide whispered their balm across the weary landscape.

Cathy sat now with her mother and father. She had one arm around them and the other across the shoulders of Tim, her fourteen-year-old son. 'Thank you, guys, for today. It's been great!'

'Slow down, love,' Peter whispered in her hair. 'Take some time for yourself. You and Rick both need space for peace in your lives. Your children still need you very much too.'

For a moment, his eyes connected with Tim. 'Send me a text,' he said to the boy. 'We have not had much time today to talk.' Tim nodded.

'Oh, Dad, life is different today. We both must be 'on call' 24/7 or we won't keep our jobs or get ahead. It's a constant treadmill, and we need money to keep the family going. I love you both very, very much. Please take care!'

'Darling.' Grace spoke for the first time. 'Guard your health and your heart. We love you dearly and only want life's very *best* for you and your family.'

James came with Barbara and sat beside Grace and Peter as cars were being loaded. 'Great lunch, Mum,' He said. 'I like the lights and the tree. I noticed you still put up the Nativity scene on top of the TV. I remember it as a child. Most people I know don't bother about that extra religious stuff.'

Grace was shocked, but Peter spoke gently and sincerely. 'Son, the secular world is rising to force its morality and lifestyles on *all* people. There is only *one* reason for the Christmas season.'

'Whatever!' James said quietly as he took Barbara's hand. 'Thank you, love you,' they called back as they drove away.

'Wait a minute please,' Grace called as the second car pulled out. She went inside and came back with a small card in her hand. 'I have something to give Lisa.'

She handed her granddaughter the card. Inside was a fragile piece of paper. 'I found it only yesterday. It is a scrap of a page from my father's diary.' He had handwritten it, and the ink was now very faint and discoloured.

Long ago, my beloved grandparents walked the cobbled streets of early Gympie. My grandfather's name was Tom Daniels, and all I clearly remember now is that he loved God.

'Perhaps this will help you with the question you asked when you were here. Who cried on the High Point many, many years ago?'

Lisa and Grace embraced through the open car window.

'Goodbyes' echoed through the trees. Car engine sounds faded into the distance. The house settled into its usual calm. Max slept on his mat.

Grace and Peter relaxed comfortably under a canopy of stars.

They breathed deeply the refreshing night-time air.

Will questions being asked, and answered, complicate or inspire the lives of this family?

CHAPTER VII

2015 Time Tunnel Journey —Finding Nika

Ten-year-old Luke Barritt burst through the verandah screen door of his Gympie Southside home. The timber floor reverberated as his slung school backpack thudded against the wall. His shoes and socks followed more quietly; only the heels of his shoes made a gentle thud as they landed.

'Dad! Dad!' he called. 'I saw the car. I'm glad you're home early.'

Lenore Barritt's voice called from the kitchen. 'Luke! Please stop shouting and charging around. Come in and have a cold drink, then tell us what's the matter.'

'Ooo, Mum.' His voice took on the desperately patient quality of his age group. 'No problem. I simply want to know something.' Grabbing a drink and a piece of chocolate cake, Luke threw himself onto the bench stool beside his father. 'Dad, have you ever heard of someone called Nika O'Reilly Barritt? She apparently lived a very long time ago.'

Through unhurried sips of coffee, Marcus thoughtfully answered, 'It's not a name I'm familiar with. Why are you interested in this person?'

39

'Mr Williams, our new history teacher, has only recently come to live in Queensland. He seems quite into Gympie history. In some library research, he read an archival file of pre-1900s writing and found several short articles with a byline "contributed by Nika O'Reilly Barritt, Gympie". He asked me about our family history and was quite excited to know we have a line of rellies dating back to probably 1880.'

'If it would help you, Luke, I'll have a word with your grandad,' Lenore said. 'Your father's dad loves to speak about the past.'

'I would ask my grandmother as well.' Derek laughed. 'She loves to tell the stories, but so much has become figments of her imagination. I've heard her share stories about James Nash, the discoverer of Gympie's gold, in 1867. She speaks as if we had family on the early goldfields. I'm certain Barritts did not come before 1880.' 'Hi, all!' The screen door slammed behind Bernadette as she joined the rest of the family. 'Gee, Dad, you're home early.'

'Well, I'll have to work hard to catch up, probably be late home for the next week now. There was a gas leak under the furniture display court, and the whole factory was shut down. Even folks like me who were trying to balance the books were ordered by the police to *go home and stay there until it's declared safe*. I've been told we should be able to return tomorrow.'

'G... r... e... a... t!' murmured Luke. He poked his sister in the ribs as she sat down beside him.

'Thanks, Mum.' Bernadette gratefully accepted the cold drink and slice of cake offered by Lenore. She ate and drank with unusual haste and was still chewing when she asked a question.

'Do we have any relatives who went to Gallipoli? We've been asked to research family World War I soldiers. Two of our former St Patrick's students have been invited to travel to Gallipoli, Fromelles, and Pozieres next year. There've been some amazing new discoveries, and many 'missing' soldiers are being identified. This team, formed from all over Australia, has been invited to bring a list of any unidentified missing with them from their local cities and towns.'

'Matthew Barritt. I've heard the story. He was one of only a few who came home again, but he would never talk about the war, and

I don't think he ever went to any of the soldiers' gatherings,' Lenore added. 'Perhaps he was a brother of your great-great-grandfather.'

'Lots of questions. I'll ring Dad and my grandmother tonight and see what help they can give.' Derek stretched and yawned. 'Anyone joining me for a run around the block?' Teenage groans were his only answer. Lenore silently followed him, and together they headed for the park.

Grandmother Stephanie phoned back. She used the landline. She did not like her mobile and fervently hoped she would not have to listen to a recorded message when she used their landline as well. Lenore tried to answer, but Stephanie gave her information in a steady stream of words without waiting for the courtesy 'hello'.

'I got your message, and I may be eighty-four, but I haven't lost my marbles yet. I do know for certain Matthew Barritt did not have any brothers – only sisters.

'Yes, he returned from WWI after spending months in a London hospital. He was my husband's dearly loved grandfather who he called Poppy. Matthew died in 1950, but I still remember his beautiful smile.

'Please tell Bernadette Matthew Barritt is direct bloodline to *all* Barritts still in Gympie. His only brother died years before he was born. I have not heard of a Nika Barritt, but my husband told me Poppy had three sisters.

'Please tell young Luke one of Matthew's sisters may be the person he's looking for.'

Armed with this new information that he had a great-great-grandfather Matthew with three sisters, he set out with these clues to find any early writings, in the archives of Nika O'Reilly Barritt. He found one paragraph. One simple paragraph, yet it answered a question.

'Mum, Dad, Bernie! I've found her! I've found her. Nika O'Reilly Barritt was adopted by Eliza and Rob Barritt way, way back when she was very young.

She wrote in an article, 'I will be forever grateful for the love shown to me by my adopted Mum and Dad – more like brother and sister than parents and for the younger brother and two sisters who always made me feel I had family.'

Steven Williams's history class was unusually excited. Many interesting stories had been discovered. 'I had a bushranger uncle,' Milly Parkinson proudly shared.

Tom Frederick's contribution brought forth a lot of discussions. 'My great-great-grandfather reckons most of early Gympie folk came either from Ireland as convicts or from foreign countries.'

Indeed, this one class revealed interesting links to European and Asian countries. There was quite astonishing global diversity.

'Luke!' His eyes searched and settled on the boy with the rumpled shirt, and flyaway ruffled hair, who was restlessly sliding back and forth across his seat. 'Luke Barritt!'

Luke looked up. *What have I done now?*

'Luke, I have discovered a bit of interesting info for you. You may like to come and check with me later if you discover anything else. Your Nika O'Reilly Barritt disappeared at the time of Gympie's big 1893 flood, but further articles in pre- WWI *Bulletin* archives showed steady contributions with the byline Nika Daniels. Gympie. I think the story of the child adopted into your family probably goes on to this day.'

Luke laughed. 'My historical research is leading me back to early Gympie streets, and my sister at high school is taking historical research into Turkey, France, and battlegrounds from the past. Could it all somehow be connected?'

'Luke, this is the reason I like history studies so much. It's a bit like a time tunnel.'

Steve walked to the front of the group. 'Please don't simply look for the information. Try and find stories of real humans with their joys, sorrows, and triumphs lived through the history in it all. For the rest of this term, gradually find stories from your folk, and we'll have a group discussion later in the year!'

'WOW,' Luke commented to his dad that night. 'It's as if I'm allowing time to travel back to find Nika Daniels. The little girl, once Nika O'Reilly Barritt. Did she stay here, or did she go? What is her story?'

Like a Time Tunnel

Gympie.

A child was born on the banks of the Mary River in 1869. An Aboriginal woman Marrangaroo and a red-haired Irish miner hugged in the darkness.

The baby's first cries rolled eerily across the surface of the water.

The three clung closely together.

Nika O'Reilly was born.

Tragically orphaned, she was adopted by friends of her father, Eliza and Robert Barritt, in 1881.

Nika O'Reilly Barritt, writer, marries Tom Daniels, evangelist pastor.

She is now Nika Daniels.

Their unfolding life story wraps around historical incidents in a developing and fast-growing community.

NIKA & TOM

Their Story

— ❧ —

After the Flood of 1893
Gympie

CHAPTER VIII

1895 – After Floods – Lives Rebuilt

The aftermath of the biggest flood in the history of the gold-mining settlement of Gympie not only left devastation but also brought seeds of great change. The 1893 flood destroyed most structures including many of the gold mines. Most were damaged beyond repair. The remaining few continued operation, and these were destined to drive the economy to peak production in 1903.

Tom Daniels stood with his wife, Nika, at the end of the still-pitted and broken remains of the main track through town called Mary Street.

Tom held their twelve-month-old son Michael proudly over his shoulder.

'Prosperity and hope for the future lie now with diversity.' He smiled as possibilities surfaced in his mind. 'The surrounding lands are being farmed, and with the timber and railway extension lines branching everywhere, talk of electricity one day and even phones, prospects ahead are astonishing.'

Nika laughed. 'Sometimes I wonder if people rise up stronger after adversity. These many shops with their new shopfronts are tributes to human hope and tenacity.'

'Oow!' She gasped as the baby reached out and clutched at the knob of her loosely rolled hair. Hair pins flew as the wind teased the golden cascade as it tumbled out. It fanned across her shoulders in waves and ripples of fire.

Tom gasped. The free-flowing life in Nika's loosened hair always evoked deep feelings in his heart. He vividly remembered the past — her beauty and his life-defining passionate love for her.

He drew her close into his arms, forming a circle around mother and son. 'Thank God we are still here. *Eliza, Rob, and their children have their new hut on the high Jakdawn ridges. We have our lovely home here in town and even the property only a few miles away. Life is certainly good!'

Nika laughed again. 'My father's legacy certainly has accomplished everything my mother believed. The hospital and children's home will become a reality in the next few years.'

'What amazes me as I stand here,' Tom continued, 'is that what began as primitive gold-diggings is now community. It has suffered much loss and has risen again. The streets are still only bullock tracks, but shops are beginning to rebuild, and people of faith are arriving from all over the world. Churches are springing up everywhere. What is the future for this place? It certainly is much more than just about gold.'

They began to walk. Tom frequently stopped. 'How are you travelling?' he enquired outside two shops where the owners were still restoring street canopies. He asked others milling around about family situations. 'Please let me know if you need anything, either prayerfully or with practical help. I'm always happy to lend a helping hand,' he called.

Most smiled and waved, shouting back a cheery greeting. There were a few who simply grunted and went about their jobs.

Less horses were tethered than a few years ago and only a few ridden now in the main street. However, some of the newer shopfronts still featured in their design a 'hitching post' at street level. Charles Barnes operated a refreshment stall from a patched-together tepee-shaped hut. He called out, 'Got time for a bit of freshly baked damper and a mug of billy tea?'

Tom and Nika happily accepted. They pulled a few boxes into a circle and sat down. They enjoyed the food and drink and this opportunity to share news and greetings from mutual friends. Tom dropped a few coins into the small can near his seat as he rose. He smiled when Charlie waved his hand to dismiss the gesture. 'We've all got to earn a living, mate. It's been great to stop for a chat.'

Michael's wriggling increased. Nika soothed him on her lap. 'He's hungry and tired. I guess we should be heading home.'

Greetings resonated from different shops and stalls as they walked, returning now on the other side of the street. Tom and Nika answered and waved. Prejudice about Nika's Aboriginal heritage had lessened as the Daniels family became an established part of the community.

Comments occasionally still surfaced. A voice spoke from the back of a large fruit-and-vegetable barrel container. 'Little'un looks like you, Tom. Bet yuh pleased he ain't got no abo features.'

It was probably meant innocently enough, intended as a jocular remark, but Nika's mind and thoughts went back to her beautiful dusky-skinned mother and her Irish dad with his tangle of bright red hair and bushy red-speckled black beard. She swiped as unexpected tears slid down her cheeks. Tom stiffened. He took a deep breath.

'Hi, everyone,' he called to the few drinkers he saw lounged at the recently reconstructed bar of the Royal Hotel.

'Merv's bull has fathered two more sets of twins,' called out a slightly slurred voice from inside.

'S'truth,' someone else confirmed.

Tom smiled and waved. 'Tell Merv I'll ride out and see them sometime soon.'

The warm sun beat on their faces and blazed on the shop awnings as the few horses tethered outside the hotel swished flies away with their tails.

Michael's restlessness intensified. He wailed a high-pitched piercing sound.

'I know, I know, you're hungry, little man,' Nika soothed. 'We won't be long now.'

'We're heading home.' Tom smiled and waved again as they turned at the upper end of Mary Street. They walked on to their pretty cottage with its green gate and window sills. It was nestled in the hillside behind the main business area.

'What a gloriously beautiful day.'

'It is, my love.' His face was animated and happy. His blue eyes sparkled, and his fair hair was tousled by the wind. Even his beard looked ruffled. 'A great day to be alive.'

She kissed his cheek, and Michael laughed as they danced inside, cradling him between them.

Gympie 1896

Robert Barritt settled in the saddle and let his mare canter along the brown road which edged the Mary riverbank to town. Eliza, Matthew, and Ellen had waved from the farmhouse veranda of their property Jakdawn. Their greetings, 'Tell Nika and Tom, we love them', still rang in his ears.

The sun was warm on his face, and he enjoyed the freedom of movement and the gentle wind through his hair and beard. He anchored his hat more securely. He didn't see the snake across the track and was grateful his mare didn't see it either and perhaps panic. The kookaburra's eyes must have picked its movements from afar. The speed with which the bird flashed down and then returned to the red gum tree was astonishing. Only the wriggling, writhing airborne snake trapped in the sharp beak gave any hint of the drama unfolding.

The snake shook itself free and began its spiralling return to earth. Robert saw it falling right on top of him, but at the very last moment, the bird again swooped and captured it in mid-air, only metres above the horse and rider.

'Flaming hell!' Robert yelled, surprised and shocked. His mare shivered violently but didn't break stride.

The morning resumed its peaceful calm. Robert's heart thumped wildly.

Nika heard the clattering hoof beats before she saw the rider. He stopped, dismounted, and tethered the brown horse to a post outside the cottage gate. She hurriedly secured the pins in her hair, wiped her hands on the pretty check apron she wore, and ran to the door.

'Rob,' she cried excitedly as she greeted him. 'It's great to see you.

I hope nothing's wrong at home.'

'No, dear, all's fine at home. They send their love. I've come to give Tom a hand with his house improvements. I know the needs with the new baby mean extensions are necessary.'

She looks so lovely. Rob's thoughts rolled on. *It took me a while to adjust to this marriage. I wanted more for her. Yet she seems very happy.*

He smiled.

Nika's golden eyes looked up into Rob's brown ones. *His black hair and beard have tiny flecks of grey.* Her thoughts too wandered. *Never a father but always, always a wonderful, caring, and loving older brother.*

'It's always wonderful to see you, Rob.' She ran into his open arms and embraced him warmly.

'We'll have a cuppa.' She put a container of water on the stove top and stirred up the coals with a poker. 'Tom's in the shed, but no doubt he's heard you ride up. The boys are still asleep, but I'm sure Michael will be out in a minute full of energy and mischief.'

'Eliza and I were delighted to hear about your new baby. Tom Jr, I believe.'

Nika nodded, and then he quietly asked, 'Do you still have time for your writing?'

'It's not easy, but yes, I still write whenever I can. The *Bulletin* in Brisbane encourages me to contribute, no matter how infrequently.'

'Try never to let it go, love, Eliza and I both believe you have a natural talent.'

'Is that you, Rob?' Tom came through the back door. 'I heard the horse and knew it must be you.'

He extended his hand. 'Great to see you, mate, and thank you so much for your offer of help with the new room and small back verandah. The timber has all been delivered, and I've started work. The two steps at the back are completed. The framework is now our major job. The cottage is very simple, and here on the hillside, well above flood height, its purpose is to be protective, durable, and provide privacy.'

'It all sounds wonderful to me.' Nika laughed happily. 'First, sit down and enjoy your cup of tea, and I'll put out the plate of biscuits.'

'Unka Rob! Unka Rob!' The small two-year-old bundle of energy burst into the room. His face, still flushed from sleep, was wreathed in cherubic smiles. His small feet were bare. A blue shirt and matching pants were crumpled and in disarray.

Tom reached down and straightened his son's clothing before handing him to Rob who hugged him and bounced him on his knee. The little boy giggled; the adults smiled.

'You can have one biscuit and a glass of milk,' Nika said seriously, 'but you must sit really, really still if you are going to stay on Uncle Rob's knee.'

They enjoyed a peaceful time around the table until the high-pitched wail of the hungry, awakening baby filled the cottage.

'I'll attend to this little one,' Nika said as she left the table. 'And you, young man, had better come with Mummy too. I'd better check you're dry and comfortable and put something on your feet.'

Tom and Rob also rose from the table. 'We'll get started on the building and see how much we can get done today.'

'Me too! Me too!' Michael suddenly ran back and pulled at Rob's pants. 'Come. Me too!' His small face with piercing blue eyes was full of entreaty.

Rob laughed. 'You go with your mother and get some shoes on, and then you can come and help us with the building.' To the surprise of everyone, he pulled a small rubber hammer from his back pocket. 'We're going to need your help if we are ever to get this job done.'

Michael ran to catch up with his mother swinging the hammer

and laughing excitedly.

Robert turned in the saddle as he wheeled the horse to ride away, and a few hours later, he looked back to wave. Tom stood with his arm around Nika and the baby, as Michael stood beside them waving furiously.

O Michael, my dear, dear friend, how proud you would be of your daughter. The child of Mangaroo – mother of future generations.

His thoughts continued as he galloped home in the cool of the late afternoon. Overhead, a flock of galahs wheeled in a screeching circle. The river far below the ridge where his house now nestled was flecked with tiny flickers of light as the setting sun slid behind the hills.

He dismounted and unlatched the top gate. 'I'm home,' he called to his waiting family.

I'll go back later in the week. It would be good to see those extensions finished.

His horse whinnied, almost as if understanding his thoughts.

CHAPTER IX

Gold Not Always Metal

A chill wind blew off the river, and the night, filled with stars, shared the soft velvet darkness of early winter. Nika sat beside the beds of her sleeping sons and comforted them with her hand. She softly sang a lullaby.

Tom paused at the door and smiled. He tiptoed to avoid making a sound, then whispered as his arms enfolded her, 'Darling, I think I'll pop down to the Salvos this evening. They have a great well-attended mid-week service. Their hall, positioned as it is, midway down the street is easily accessible. I'll enjoy the walk as the extra gaslight at the end of the street will make their entrance easier to find. I don't expect to be late home.'

'I look forward to coming with you when the babies are a bit older.' She blew him a farewell kiss.

Mary Street was crowded. The three hotels and two brothels attracted a constant crowd of people. The night was surprisingly noisy.

Tom slipped quietly into a seat. The small hall vibrated with sound as a brass band played from the back. Hymn sheets were

51

passed, and folks began to sing enthusiastically.

Sounds of drunken revelry from outside increased considerably in volume. The band played on undeterred.

Belligerent curses, with thuds and groaning indications of fighting and other assorted noises, came closer.

Suddenly, a section of the crowd burst through the door. Jeering and laughing, they chanted obscenities and drowned out the singing with discordant raucous songs of their own.

The major turned to his lieutenant. 'We'll need to sort this out,' he said quietly.

'I stayed inside with the rest of the congregation and tried to keep the flow of the meeting going,' Tom later shared with Nika.

'Noises outside were violent and very loud. We heard vile language and lots of threshing about and knew fists were finding targets. Then words of prayer began to ebb and flow. There was rhythm and harmony. A strange unnatural silence came over everything. The band stopped playing. Inside the hall, we sat very still. I saw a faint golden glow through the open door.

'Then the major followed by the lieutenant returned to the meeting. He wiped a smear of blood from his face and commented, "It was as if the devil raged outside this place tonight. All hell broke loose in the street. The men were filled with spirits – not Holy Spirit – and then in the middle of mayhem, at the height of the battle, suddenly it was as if the Holy Ghost turned up. Thirteen souls repented of their sins and gave their lives to Christ. A brawl turned into a prayer meeting. Hallelujah! Let's all sing 'Amazing Grace'."

'People kept streaming through the door. The hall was packed. It was a truly wonderful meeting!'

'What actually happened outside?' Nika's animated face was alight with interest. 'Did you see anything at all?'

'No. I couldn't see outside. I was aware of the incredible stillness and the soft glow that suddenly was on the ceiling and walls inside. I know that a riot turned into stillness, and inside we were swamped by a feeling of God's Presence and Peace.'

True stories become legends in small towns.

Nika and Tom would share the story through the years with their expanding family. Their lives are destined to contain many significant events, and among them will be more golden memories.

CHAPTER X

Gympie 1903 – The Daniels Family – Growing Up

'Golden Fairy Sparkles'

The sound of children's laughter reverberated around the walls of the extended cottage on Nash Street.

Nine-year-old Michael and seven-year-old Tom wrestled like puppies on the mat. They were each trying to claim possession of a battered blue object. 'It's my hat!' Tom cried passionately.

'I thought it was a duster.' Michael laughed as he grabbed it again and waved it triumphantly. 'Got it!'

Four-year-old Beth held the hand of her three-year-old sister Maree, and together they occasionally pushed and shoved at the squirming bodies of their brothers on the floor. They laughed, with the high-pitched, giggling enthusiasm of very young children.

The front door suddenly opened.

'Daddy! Daddy!' Bodies unrolled, and four figures flung themselves at the man silhouetted in the doorway.

54

Tom looked exhausted. His face was pale and coated with dust, his hair tousled and windblown. When he removed his hat, there was a red mark across his forehead.

He sighed.

'Hello there, you young rascals.' He hugged each child and planted a kiss on individual heads. They clustered around him and hugged his knees. He was unable to move.

Nika came from the back room. Her green dress swirled across the floor as she ran to greet him. Her face was radiant – her golden eyes shone. Her hair was tied back from her face with a black ribbon. 'Darling, I didn't hear you ride in. Did you leave the horse in the stable down the road?'

'Yes, I paid the boy to care for her and give her a comfortable and safe few days. It's been a long, tiring couple of weeks.'

She ran into his open arms and said quietly and gently to the children, 'Go now and draw some pictures, then we'll all have lunch together.

'Tom, darling, we've missed you. I hope you were able to help and all is well.'

He kissed her passionately. 'Dear one, I've missed you too. All is well with the MacArthurs or as well as they can be in the circumstances.

'We found Steve's body as well as the bodies of his workmen. The horses have been recaptured, and most of the cattle are contained again in the fenced paddocks. No one is certain about what caused the stampede, but police are investigating as there were reports of unknown horsemen in the hill country, and rifle fire. I stayed with the MacArthurs and helped with the milking for a few days. New workmen have been employed, so the family are slowly getting back to normal. I'm grateful to our small community. Help with aid parcels came from all over the place. The Catholics sent an aid bundle, the Church of England – a parcel. The Salvos and Methodists all contributed both manpower and aid. A lot of compassion and care came from the heart of the community.'

Tom reached out and held Nika's hand. 'Let us pray now together, dear, for comfort and peace for those who are grieving.

Amen.'

Tom recovered well after a hot bath, an afternoon sleep, and the normal resumption of his daily family life.

The cattle rustlers were never caught, but one hundred animals were reported stolen in a three-month period.

Tom gathered his family together one night, a few weeks later. 'Nika, I'm not sure about your feelings on this, but it's been in my heart for some weeks. I would like us, as a family, to make a "faith" declaration perhaps in the small Methodist Church at the bottom of Surface Hill. Life is unpredictable. It could be a simple service of commitment and faith to unite us as a family.'

Nika smiled her radiant smile. 'Yes, Tom, I think that would be a good idea. It's like a thanksgiving for us and our children... Michael, Tom, Beth, and Maree.'

He laughed. 'Yup. A kinda gratitude expression for what we have.'

It was a morning of brilliant sunshine. The sky overhead was startling blue with white fluffy clouds splayed like a canvas of shifting life across the horizon. Parrots screeched overhead then nestled noisily in gum trees lining the back roads.

Mary Street stretched before them as the family walked, with arms linked, from their home and turned in to the main thoroughfare. Recent paving of the streets had transformed the main area. No longer bullock track ridges, but now smooth and flat.

'Daddy, look!' Beth pointed. 'Fairy sparkles.'

They stopped. Every eye was captured by what was before them. As the sunlight poured onto the newly paved roads, pin-pricks of golden lights danced up and down the street.

'Oh, Nika,' Tom gasped. 'They used the mullock heaps waste from the mines to pave the streets. The streets are literally paved with gold.' Tom and Nika laughed. The boys stood very still, stunned. The two little girls danced, pretending to be fairies.

The direction of the sun shifted, and the moment was gone.

The family continued their walk to the base of Surface Hill where the small wooden structure of the Methodist Church nestled into the hillside.

'This day we affirm our commitment to the One who is Higher than ourselves. We surrender our lives into His Keeping. In Jesus name, amen.'

The congregation and the minister pronounced their prayers of faith and agreement. Everyone bowed their heads. 'Amen.'

Like golden rain, the sparkles turned the street into a river of gold.

CHAPTER XI

1905 – A City – Gold – Growth

White feathery clouds drifted across the blue canopy of January sky. The full heat from the summer sun was tempered but would rise in intensity as the clouds dispersed. Birds called as they swooped and darted from tree to tree. They would gradually settle and become less active as the day warmed.

'Please slow down a bit, boys. Remember little Maree can't walk as fast as you.'

Nika moved with leisurely grace along the dusty, grass-fringed track. The hem of her grey dress swished through the grass and dust as, hand in hand with her two small daughters, she skipped along. Their black-booted feet stirred swirls of dust in the slight morning breeze. Nika's hair was only loosely tied back and freely swung in golden ripples across her shoulders.

'They're still going too fast!' Maree wailed. She sat down. Her grey bonnet slipped over her face, and her school satchel thudded to the ground. 'I'm not walking any further.'

The two boys stopped. Eleven-year-old Michael turned and ran back, laughing. He scooped up the school bag and grabbed her hand. 'Come on, sis, not far to go now. If you're really going to be a schoolgirl today, then this is where we'll walk every day. You'll get used to it... Wait for us, Tom. We'll walk the last bit through the paddock together.'

The Daniels family entered the grounds of One Mile School through an open heavy timber gate. Several horses were already tethered along the fence line under the shade of overhanging trees. They jostled and snorted as the family passed.

Mavis Granthorpe greeted them on the timber verandah of the schoolhouse. 'Good to see you, boys.' She smiled at Michael and Tom. 'Now, we have your two sisters as well. Welcome, Beth and Maree.'

The two girls shuffled and shyly snuggled closer into Nika. 'I wasn't sure about Maree,' Nika said quietly. 'She's still very young. She won't be five until May but was so keen to come with the others.'

Mavis laughed. Her coiled bun of black hair shook wildly. She was still in her late thirties but appeared older. Maturity had come with the rapid expansion of the school. From its early gold rush beginnings in 1869, it now stretched across the open paddock with separate buildings for girls and infants, the boys being taught in their own building at the end of the wing which had been added in 1884.

'She's old enough to join us, if you have evidence to prove their respective ages.'

'Beth is already six.' Nika placed papers on the timber table. She smiled at each of her children and drew Maree a little closer to her side. 'Our youngest here is still only four.'

Nika thoughts went back to her father's struggle to get her enrolled in the first government school, and she was ten before he could get her a place. *Because my mother was Aboriginal, it was very difficult. It's great to see many dusky children's faces in the playground. Our children should blend without prejudice here now!*

A bell rang somewhere further along the verandah, and Mr Conrad appeared. He clapped his hands. 'Boys!' he called. 'Form two straight lines and follow me.' With military precision, they marched behind their teacher across the playground and up the steps into the classroom. 'Prayers first and then into some work,' Stan Conrad barked. Michael and Tom waved to Nika. Nika waved back as their two figures disappeared among the mix of assorted-sized boys.

Thoughts clearly formed in her mind. *How close they are. Michael with his head of dark hair and Tom Jr sandy-blond like his father. Marching side by side up the steps and into school. Our two dearly loved sons.*

Mavis spoke suddenly. 'Oh! I'm sorry, Mrs Daniels, I didn't mean to startle you. Would you like to see Beth and Maree settled now with the other girls in their room?' Nika followed her from the small office into the next room. There were rows of wooden desks with slates and slate pencils neatly stacked in every place. Maree and Beth looked very small at the front with the older girls of different ages in the seats behind. They smiled when she gently kissed the top of each head.

At least they look happy. An unexpected tear ran down her cheek.

She wiped it away.

'You can stay for a while, if you like,' Mavis said quietly.

'Thank you, but I should go home if the girls are settled. Tom has been at some sort of community meeting, and I told him I'd be back as soon as everyone was ready for classes.'

She waved, and several girls waved back.

'I'll be back to walk home with you.' She smiled at Beth and Maree, and they grinned.

The walk back across the green paddocks and along the dusty connecting roads in the summer sunshine was the loneliest Nika had felt for many years. *All the children now at school. How fast the years have flown!*

She lifted her skirt and ran with hot tears coursing down her cheeks. She slowed in the final five hundred yards and then with dignity and grace walked sedately onto the main street. She smiled and greeted folks she knew at the stalls and in the shopfronts and finally turned the corner and entered her cottage home on the hillside behind Mary Street.

Tom met her at the door. He hugged her enthusiastically. She could tell he was bursting with news, but first he asked, 'Is everything all right with the children?'

When she nodded, he rushed on, 'As you know, on Thursday 5 January, Gympie was officially declared a city. Our population has exploded because of the gold and the mining, but there is a bit of unrest in the community. Everyone's thrilled we're on the map now with city status and will have an official mayor but are wondering about increased taxes for ordinary folks.

'I think it's a great sign of a tremendous future for us, and I hope everyone will support the mayor and his council and all work towards this future together.'

**Mayor Garricks's official robe arrived in March. The garment was constructed of black peau de soie silk, lined with satin and trimmed with sable fur with a real Maltese collarette. The mayor wondered if this valuable city asset should be safely stored and ordered a handsome wardrobe, with a full-length mirror on the front.

'He's going to wear it for an official function to celebrate the city status of Gympie,' Tom later shared with Nika, 'then will carefully put it away in the cupboard. There's not much news in the *Gympie Times* about us becoming a city either mainly because there is so much happening with our gold production. Truly, for a rural community, we're really experiencing extraordinary diversity and change.'

Nika laughed. 'We've got a family to care for. I guess keeping us all fed, clothed, educated, and nurtured is all we are really able to do.'

'Let's never forget the spiritual either,' Tom commented seriously. 'Life must not be allowed to focus obsessively on the here and now but always for more of the sacred and meaningful aspect of our futures.'

Nika laughed again, moved closer, and kissed him. 'Limga, darling.

Eternal... lasting. The past and future rock solid with hope.'

After School... Sharing of Gold Story . . .

'Mum! Mum!' One afternoon, the silence of the Nash Street cottage was shattered as the four Daniels children came bursting through the door.

They flung their bags on the floor and with a tangled jumble of legs and arms embraced their mother. She laughed and pointed to the table. 'Good to see you all.' She hugged them passionately. 'But let's sit down and have a drink and piece of cake.'

Tom spoke first. 'Mum, Mr Conrad told us a story today of something that happened in Gympie's early gold history. Do you and Dad know if it's true?'

Michael added, 'Mr Conrad told us it is true but a bit hush-hush because of taxes and stuff in the past.'

The boys shared the story while Nika and the girls listened attentively.

'Well, apparently two men worked a shaft of a gold reef called Lady Mary. They filled two holes with explosives one afternoon and then went off for their supper. When they came back, slowly and quite uncaring, they stopped amazed. The walls of their claim were covered with gold. The walls looked like pure gold! They had to sit up all night to guard the place in case someone else saw their find.

When the stone was put through the battery, solid gold had to be chiselled from between the stampers.'

'Whatever that means,' Tom interjected. 'We just wrote it down.'

Michael added, 'On that same night, the wife of one of the partners gave birth to a son.'

'Pure gold!' Tom emphasised. 'Not strips or nuggets but a wall of solid gold.' His eyes widened with excitement. 'It actually happened in this place!'

'What did they call the baby?' Maree asked eagerly.

'I wonder if he's someone we know who still lives here,'

Beth added.

The boys groaned. 'The story was about solid gold walls and all you girls can think about is babies. GIRLS! HUH!'

Nika laughed. 'It's a great story. I'll ask your dad about it, but for now you do homework and go out and play until tea time. Be grateful you're not helping with milking or working as hard as your dad is this week with milking, fencing, and railway yard chores.'

I'm grateful too. Nika's happy thoughts spiralled. *Tom is encouraging me to spend time writing. What joy! To have a little more time for this and also the opportunity to keep writing contact with Edith in England. Her friendship since she first wrote means a lot to me. We share a deep heart connection, and I know because she has no children she loves to hear about our life here as a family.*

A jangling, ringing sound came from the shiny black box with its wind-up dialling handle and mouthpiece cradle. 'The telephone?' Nika reached for the handpiece. Although the telephone connections had been put through in 1901, many on the outskirts of town were still without the facility.

'Hello!'

'Nika, it's Eliza. Isn't this weird! We only got a phone today. It's like a miracle talking to you like this. Are you and Tom and the children keeping well?'

Nika still found it hard to communicate with the inanimate object in her hand and simply said into the mouthpiece. 'Yes. Hope you, Rob, and your family are too.'

They said goodbye, and Nika returned to her writing. *Strange to speak with my dear foster mum in such a stilted manner. I don't think I like this new telephone thing.*

It was dark and late when Tom returned home. The children were in bed. He dropped exhausted into a chair. 'Had to round up some more stolen cattle,' he commented. Rustlers are still raiding the properties around town… oops city.' He sighed and yawned.

After dinner, he relaxed. He was finishing his cup of tea when Nika told him the story of the golden walls. He confirmed it as a truth one of the mining experts had shared with him. 'I have a feeling much of the history of this place will be lost in the fast pace of rapid growth. It's only the people's stories which will last through the centuries.'

They sat together looking up into the dark night sky. The star constellation of the Southern Cross was clearly visible against the black backdrop of the autumn evening. 'Nika, darling, let's always be grateful for what we have.' He bowed his head. *Father, grant us all peace and rest this night, in Jesus name, amen.*

Across the sky, an owl hooted as it roamed, its huge round eyes piercing the darkness hunting for food.

The house settled, and a family slept.

CHAPTER XII

Empire Day – 24 May 1911

The small community gathering of citizens in the city hall reception area clapped as the mayor walked onto the platform.

'Ladies and gentlemen, Empire Day, the birthday remembrance of Her Late Majesty Queen Victoria, is celebrated in all Queensland state schools. They enjoy their half-day holiday. Now that Edward VII's coronation is to be celebrated, the date may be changed to 9 August. However, children are assured their half-day holiday will remain.'

The assembled students clapped enthusiastically.

'It is now my pleasure to announce that Maree Daniels from One Mile State School has won a certificate in the Empire Day State Schools Essay Competition. Maree, would you please come forward now.'

Tom took Nika's hand. 'Memories of your winning story, so long ago. History is repeating itself.' She smiled and wordlessly squeezed his hand.

Shyly, Maree took the certificate from the mayor's hand. She looked small and a bit scared standing beside him in his impressive

65

regalia.

'I would like you to read a small section please.' The mayor indicated a marked paragraph as he handed her a copy of her winning entry. The child with the elfin face and dark hair and dressed in a pale-blue floor-length linen-weave dress moved to the front of the platform.

Clearly and confidently she read,

'We should be proud of our school, our community, and our country, Australia.

We should be proud too that we belong to a whole lot of other countries which are part of the British Empire. We are proud of our former Queen… Victoria and glad her son Edward is now our crowned King.

Empire Day is a good day to celebrate all our blessings.'

To rousing cheers and claps, Maree returned to her seat at the side of the platform.

'Time for lunch,' the mayor announced heartily. 'Plenty of sandwiches and cake for all.' His hand passed like a benediction over the heads of the gathered students as he added, 'Then, after lunch, everyone can go home.' He laughed. 'Except me. Still got lots of work on my desk in the city hall. Seems appropriate,' he added with a chuckle. 'Now that our local chap Andrew Fisher is back as prime minister, a city hall for us seems more appropriate than a town hall.'

The passion and loyalty to the ideals of empire and the sworn oaths of allegiance to God, King, and country were part of ordinary life in most Australian communities. Gympie's younger generation were inspired to take their part and prove their manhood, if, in the future, it became necessary to maintain these ideals. This they certainly did!

CHAPTER XIII

1912 – Whip-cracking and a Girl Called Erin

The green paddock sprawled into the distance alive with the dazzling brilliance of spring sunshine.

A cluster of sulkies parked in careless disarray under the cluster of trees had an abandoned appearance. Horses roamed the top paddocks safely enclosed by a rocky escarpment and a section of high fence.

The chatter of human voices resonated in the afternoon air. The occasional sharp crack of a stock whip sent the bird population spiralling into the blue sky. Soft fluffy clouds floated in gentle serenity on a light breeze. The smell of spring was evident. Aromas from wattle, wild flowers, and gum leaves subtly blended with still-damp grass, carried across from the distant river, and caressed the senses.

Robert Barritt looked across the heads of the congregated young people and smiled at his wife, Eliza.

This picnic for the youngsters has surely worked out well. I'm glad this railway land is still so securely fenced yet remains quite natural. It's ideal for an open day.

His thoughts were interrupted by Eliza's call. 'Rob, young Tom's

67

going to try a bit of whip cracking.'

Rob carefully navigated his way around the spread of picnic rugs and baskets and joined the others at the fenced corral area where several young men were lining up to 'give it a go.'

Nika and Tom stood at the fence across the corral from the Barritts. They waved. Michael, Beth, and Maree were somewhere with their cousins among the chattering youthful group of interested spectators.

'First time I've tried in public,' Tom Jr grinned. His flushed face under the large black hat, and the confined swagger of his jodhpurs and cowboy boots, gave him an air of cheeky confidence.

He lifted the whip with his right hand and, with a flick of his wrist, smiled as it cracked and made a circle in the air. Then he brought it down, and it thrashed the ground with a snaking moving motion which teased the spiralling dust.

Embarrassed now, Tom backed out the corral gate, trailing the whip behind him.

'Good on yuh, young Tom. Not a bad effort for yuh first go,' someone called.

As others came, one by one, to take their turn, Tom saw Erin McCarthy. She walked towards him with surprising grace for a fifteen-year-old girl. The hem of her long skirt brushed the tops of booted feet. The face under the lace trim of her sun bonnet was delicately flushed. 'Well done, Tom,' she said shyly. 'I'm proud you gave it such a good go.'

He touched her hand. 'Thanks.'

Nika remarked to Tom Sr, 'Those two are very good friends. I hope they'll learn and live a bit before they think of anything more serious.' 'I hope he's as lucky as I've been. My love for you, Nika, is as strong as it ever was when we were young.'

She punched his arm. 'Poor old bloke. Speak for yourself. I'm still young.'

The copper lights in her golden eyes looked up at him, and he felt the familiar 'heart tug' as sunlight played with loose strands of her golden hair flying free from under her large hat.

'Let's go and finish our picnic now. I guess the young'uns will prefer to be with their friends instead of eating with the aged.' He kissed Nika's forehead and did a little jig.

Rob and Eliza joined them, and they walked together to where the picnic rugs and baskets of food and drinks waited.

It was a gloriously beautiful spring day with no hint of the storm clouds of war gathering on distant horizons.

CHAPTER XIV

1913–1918 Flashpoints – A World Shaken

Winds of unrest and change swept across Europe as the world moved into the twentieth century.

Struggles for power dominated centre stage. The war between France and Prussia led to a humiliating defeat for France and the creation of a powerful German Empire. Alliances formed between nations endeavouring to strengthen their ties. Great Britain formed an alliance with France which already had an alliance with Russia. This triple 'entente' became the core of World War I allies.

In an endeavour to destabilise this three-cord alliance, tensions erupted. The Moroccan Crisis, the Tangier Crisis, and the Agadir Crisis were all ripples designed to shake the core. Instead of 'softening' these links, it only produced increased hostility towards Germany.

Then fires of 'unrest' in rapid succession were lit in Central Europe. Austria/Hungary decided to annex Bosnia/Herzegovina. Bitterness enraged Serbia, and the humiliated Russian government determined they would not suffer in similar fashion.

The Italian-Turkish War in 1911 did not threaten European peace, but it revealed the weakness of the Ottoman army and raised issues of vast territorial ownership to be gained from this decaying Ottoman Empire.^{***}

All these distant disputes and rumblings were far removed from rural Australia and little filtered through to disturb the peace of normal life within this distant outpost of the British Empire.

Then the Austrian-Hungarian heir presumptive and his wife were assassinated by Bosnian 'conspirators'. This detonated events which ignited other events, leading to the world's first global war: World War I.

Austria-Hungary presented an ultimatum to Serbia – from Vienna came impossible demands. Then Austria-Hungary unleased full military might and invaded Serbia. Russia mobilised in support of Serbia.

Germany attacked neutral Luxembourg on 2 August and on 3 August declared war on France. On 4 August Belgium refused to permit German troops to cross its borders into France. Germany responded by declaring war on Belgium as well.

Britain declared war on Germany on 4 August (effective at 11pm) after no agreement was reached that Belgium be kept neutral.

This swept all the dominions within the British Empire – India, Canada, South Africa, New Zealand, and Australia – into the conflagration of a catastrophic world situation.

In Australia when war was officially declared, there was little need for recruitment. Young men came from everywhere – farms, towns, communities – to play their part. The powerful call of service to God, King, and country brought them on foot, on horseback. Many walked miles from remote towns in the outback to connect with rail lines, and carriages were always full.

The Daniels family gathered in their newly built hut at Hillrock, on their property in the Gympie hinterland.

'These few days together will be good for us all.' Tom's smile encompassed everyone, but his expression was strained.

Nika stared at the faces gathered around the long table. She looked unnaturally pale. 'Please don't tell me all three of you are going to enlist. Not all three men in our family. Please no!' Tears splashed onto the tabletop, and Beth and Maree moved to sit closer to their mother.

Tom instantly moved around the table and hugged her passionately to his side. 'Darling, I'm so sorry I have not had the time to let you know what has been going on. Yes, I admit I felt at first I should enlist as well as our sons. Indeed, that it was a duty and responsibility. Yet as I prayed, I sensed a challenge that there will be many needs here in the community, and I have a job to do and need to remain.

'Even when I heard Andrew Fisher's declaration that Australia's commitment was to "help and support the mother country to her last man and last shilling", my heart was stirred, yet there was a deeper spiritual certainty of a calling to remain. I will be here in town with you and the girls, but perhaps I will be called to many and various places where my help could lighten the burden caused by absent farm workers and families.'

He kissed Nika's forehead and ran his hand tenderly across her shoulders. 'I'll be here, my love. It's in the Will of God I stay.'

Michael and Tom Jr had sat side by side silently observing as Nika and Tom Sr conversed. Both hated the distress on their mother's face but were grateful their father understood they did not wish to leave but *knew* it was something duty required of them.

Then Tom Jr spoke. His voice resonated with anxiety but also with excitement. 'Mum, Dad, I have asked Erin to be my wife. We're planning to be married next week. I've arranged with the reverend from the Methodist Surface Hill Church to conduct the service on Tuesday in the late afternoon. He has agreed as Erin has turned seventeen and I am eighteen. We will have a short honeymoon at Tin Can Bay. I'll have a couple of days back in Gympie to complete enlistment details and be ready for the train journey on 24 August to our training camp in Brisbane.'

He grinned at Michael. 'Sorry to keep it a secret from you, brother, but everything's just happened incredibly fast. I'd be happy if you'll be best man.'

Michael laughed. 'You've shocked me. I had no idea, but yes, I would be delighted to be best man.'

Tom now anxiously scanned his parents' faces and was relieved to see their smiles.

Nika spoke first. 'You're very young, darling. It's not what we normally would have wanted, but Erin's a lovely girl. We hope you'll be very happy. She'll ensure a welcome home when this war is over.' Tom at her side added quietly, 'Since her gran died, I know she's been very lonely. We certainly do welcome her warmly into our family.'

'While you're away, I hope she'll stay with us,' Nika added. 'We'd love to have her as she plans what will be needed for your future home together.'

'Mum, Dad, thank you for understanding. Your prayers and love will always give me strength and certainty until I return. Than… k you.' His blue/green eyes suddenly flooded with tears. Nika ran to hold him as she pulled Michael closer as well. Memories of her two sons and their childhood days flooded her mind.

Beth and Maree joined the circle, and Tom moved to stand behind and tried to embrace them all. His heart was overwhelmed with love for his family, and he was unable to speak. He simply lifted his eyes, and there was a silent prayer in his heart.

The Wedding

The winter afternoon still had chill in the air as the Daniels family walked from their home to the Methodist Manse in Reef Street. Sunlight warmed and played across their excited faces.

Eliza and Robert Barritt parked their sulky and freed their horse in the paddock behind the Nash Street house.

'We'll walk with you,' Eliza called as she grabbed Robert's arm, held up the hem of her dragging skirt, and ran with him to catch up with the others.

Michael and Tom Jr walked arm in arm as carefree as children on a beach. There was no hint of warfare or conflict on their faces. Their khaki uniforms made a subdued honour guard as the others, in their colourful clothing, walked behind.

Nika wore emerald green, her most flattering colour. Her hair rippled with golden lights even as the sun disappeared behind a cloud. The sinking sun still had enough light to shimmer on the pastel-coloured dresses worn by Beth and Maree. With matching golden-brown shoulder wraps, their youthful dance-like movements swirled their skirts along the pavement, as shafts of this light played across their faces, making their eyes sparkle.

Tom Sr waited with Erin on the small verandah. The idea of this service on the Manse verandah had been the reverend's. 'A commitment and promises made under the night sky. Simple but very beautiful.'

He smiled warmly when Tom Sr moved aside and gently placed Erin's hand on Tom's arm as his son reached the top step. He then joined the others.

Michael stood behind his brother, and the rest of the family assembled in a quiet and reverent circle surrounding them.

'I take you, Tom . . .' 'I take you, Erin.'

The reverend's voice clearly reverberated. 'I now pronounce you husband and wife. May the Lord God be the Strength and the Guidance in your union, as long as you both shall live. Amen.'

Gympie August 1914

Great news of railway tenacity and achievement came. The long-awaited line to the Mary Valley as far as Kandanga was complete! The excitement of this long-envisioned accomplishment sadly was overshadowed now by war news.

Enthusiastic crowds attended the mayor's farewell speech to the thirty-three Gympie volunteers joining the Australian Expeditionary Force.

Michael and Tom stood smartly 'to attention' with the others lined up, behind the lorry, draped with a Union Jack. The mayor and two aldermen sat on this platform.

Behind the gathered volunteers were the Light Horsemen and

infantry. The general public with its usual mix of town folk, miners, farmers, railway workers, consisted of family groups, excited children and jostling, interested visiting relatives. This wall of people extended back down Mary Street and overflowed into the streets on each side.

The mayor rose to his feet. His speech was short but sincere. 'We care about each person gathered here and know you will conduct yourselves with dignity always upholding the honour of the Union Jack and all it represents.'

From the piano located near the platform, the strains of 'Rule, Britannia' wafted. The clear strong voice of a respected local tenor began to sing, and the throbbing refrain reverberated down the streets as the crowd picked up the chorus.

24 August

The train slowly gathered pace as it pulled away from Gympie Station. Suddenly, there was no time left for more words. Time suddenly appeared suspended, but also raced. Erin ran beside the train. Tom reached to touch her hand. How they both wished this moment had never come. Beth and Maree, faces tear-stained, waved frantically as their two brothers pressed against a train window.

Families were desperate for one final glimpse as loved ones began now the journey south for military training at Enoggera.

Nika and Tom stood at the end of the platform as the train disappeared into the distance. They stood silent and still. When Erin, Beth, and Maree joined them, they let the warmth of the sunshine and gentle spring breeze play across their faces. All along the station platform, family groups huddled, gaining strength from one another.

The time of waiting for loved ones to return had begun.

1915

'The railway line has reached Brooloo,' Robert Barritt called as he entered the kitchen at Jakdawn. Eliza smiled as she turned from the stove. 'What a wonderful goal now achieved.'

'It's a bit sad. The war news is so grim it dominates everything.

Even the *Gympie Times* has its main story today, 'Call to Arms'.'

He walked across the room and took her into his arms. 'We are living in such tragic times. There's no space anymore for any good news.'

They stood silently together, remembering their own son Matthew and all the hundreds of thousands of young men far away on foreign battle fields.

Absence

Grief and 'absence' affected not only the human population. Mothers, fathers, sisters and brothers, families, and friends all suffered. The unseen and rarely acknowledged loss was experienced by animals. On small farms and properties, through townships and cities and relatively unknown pockets of development, many dogs waited for masters. Horses grazing in sun-kissed paddocks looked into the distance and wondered where their riders had gone. Some would never again know the freedom of open spaces with the child and then the young man upon their backs. Grief is not always visible, but in some small communities, the pain of missing young folk was poignantly real.

In Gympie, it was the silent companion in the lives and visible on the faces of a whole community.

Yet hope for the future was also evident.

On the cold winter mornings of early June 1915, many babies were born in Gympie. Several private maternity nursing homes, formerly family homes, had been given or leased to a team of qualified nursing sisters. This enabled them to provide first-class comfort and care.

On June 2, in Kingston House, Michael Robert Daniels protested vehemently at the disruption to his peace as the violent contractions of his mother's body brought his life into the world. His loud bellow was heard by passers-by. The attending sister laughed.

After a long labour, Erin was exhausted. Tears streamed down her face. 'Tom, Tom,' she sobbed. 'How I wish you could be here. Will you be home soon? We've had no mail since your letters from the training camp in Egypt.'

Nika and Tom Sr sat beside their daughter-in-law. Tom took her hand and prayed a silent prayer for *peace*. Nika and Erin embraced. The women found comfort in their shared love for one young soldier, among many, so far away.

Nika stroked Erin's hair and sponged her hot perspiring face.

Tom gathered them into his arms, and the flailing hands of the new baby brushed against his hand. It was very gentle – a simple touch – but something deep in Tom's heart stirred.

'O God,' he prayed aloud. 'Be with us all. No matter what the future may be, we need Your Strength. Amen.'

CHAPTER XV

Gympie – War Years – 1916/17

A grim-faced crowd gathered at the city hall as the mayor shuffled through his sheaf of papers.

'No good news I'm afraid, folks,' he said. 'War news is limited. Very little is ever released about the progress of the war, but an increasingly disturbing number of Australian deaths are being confirmed. Four from this area have been confirmed as among the dead, but many others are still missing.

'Sorry, Tom,' he called when he saw Tom Daniels move among people offering support and comfort to the recipients of the latest shattering news. 'Nothing at all about Michael and Tom. They are simply listed as still 'missing'.'

The winter winds of 2016 blew strongly in Mary Street, but external cold barely registered as a community tried to balance work and normalcy with constant hope and mind-numbing uncertainty.

Nika threw herself with focused intensity into her writing with short articles being accepted by the *Sydney Bulletin*. She also kept up a lengthy and detailed correspondence with Edith in the UK. They gleaned comfort from the honesty of the exchanges between them.

Both Beth and Maree had regular jobs. They were employed in local shops but were also ready to assist in home situations where mothers and children struggled.

Tom was rarely at home. 'I'm sorry, darling,' he said on one occasion. 'Every day I ride out of town I find someone who needs help. Trying to find pickers for crops and help with milking, branding, and property maintenance is becoming increasingly difficult. The war has taken away more than the kids from the cities but has decimated the available workforce on many properties. Last week I was offered two jobs — permanent on the railways — I had to refuse but will try and spread myself out to help where I possibly can.'

Nika hugged him. 'I know, love, you would work for nothing, but your labours are valued and the income helps.' She planted a kiss on the top of his head. 'Come home when you can, and stay safe.'

He called back as he mounted and rode away. 'Erin and the baby are loving it at Hillrock. She's got two friends with babies staying there at present. They love the peace and certainly are a support to one another. She'll be back in town in a few days.'

1917

The Kenilworth State School burnt to the ground. Not long after, the Alliance Hotel was reduced to smouldering rubble.

'Have you noticed all the news about fires?' Tom remarked as the family walked home from a morning service at the Methodist Church. 'Sorrow and helplessness are very often expressed in unexpected ways.'

He was even more deeply disturbed when the son of a family he knew well was caught, actually lighting a fire, at Central State School. The Fire Brigade were frustrated that lack of water pressure meant another school could not be saved.

On a warm and pleasant day in the early summer of 1917, when scudding clouds of purest white brought movement and life to the strikingly blue sky, all fires, underlying unease, and distress became stark reality.

The mayor made an announcement to the assembled crowd. His voice was choked with emotion, and his hands shook.

'I have been informed by the War Office today that official confirmation has come that classified "missing" Australian soldiers are now listed as "missing but are *all* presumed dead". I'm so very sorry for each one of you who hoped for better news.'

His eyes scanned the faces, desperately looking for Tom.

Tom stood on the very edge of the crowd locked in an embrace with his wife, daughters, daughter-in-law, and squirming, restless grandson and felt his life shatter into pieces. Grief twisted his heart like a knife wound. A sob threatened to rise and choke him.

Yet he saw the mayor's nod and knew he had to say or do something… Pray.

This is a bit like the days in the past when I was an evangelist on the street. Thoughts swirled, round and round.

His voice, when it finally came, was unexpectedly and powerfully clear. He swallowed. *Father God, help me!*

'Because our Lord Jesus Christ rose from death and ascended into heaven and His instruction to His followers forever *is* 'Follow Me', I have the Hope and Faith to believe that one day we also will go where our sons have gone beyond the sunset, beyond all suffering and pain.'

Sobbing resonated down Mary Street and echoed eerily from shopfronts. Groups of people clung together, swamped by grief and an all-consuming sense of loss.

Tom prayed.

Father God. We need Your Strength. We need Your Healing. Help us to grieve but never to lose our Hope for this community and the lives we are to live.

We ask, O Lord, that one day the places where the 'missing' lie — where only You know now — will all *be found. In Jesus' name. Amen.* Tom moved back into the embrace of his family, and together they walked to connect with other groups. The community mourned the loss of a generation of young men. These missing links in the 'life' chain could not be replaced. Nor could holes in the fabric of family ever be mended.

Shared grief was the 'living' reality which carried them forward during these dark and difficult days.

———⚜———

Hillrock (Nika's Deep Grief)

The small two-roomed timber hut looked tiny among the cluster of large white gum trees. The water in the dam sparkled as rays from the rising sun reflected on the ripples caused by hungry catfish hunting below.

Nika touched Tom's shoulder. He muttered in his sleep. She gently kissed his forehead. 'I'm off for a walk. Won't be long.'

Nika had used part of her father's ongoing life provision[****] to purchase Hillrock (a cut-off section from a massive cattle property) in 1910.

Not really suitable for farming, but certainly a small pocket of countryside where animals and birds can find sanctuary. Maybe a legacy, for future generations. Her thoughts spiralled. A choking sob rose in her throat Clear of the dam site, she let down her hair. It cascaded wildly with golden ripples of unrestrained abandon. It splayed across her shoulders and down her back. Lifting the hem of her trailing skirt, she wrapped it, tied it, then anchored it with the huge hair clip, securely on her hip. With her legs freer now, she moved quickly. Booted feet pounded a determined staccato on the rocky surface of the narrow, cleared road.

Composure was completely gone. Tears streamed down her face as she climbed the steep incline and reached the small flat area at the high point. Tom had already carved the primitive beginnings of a seat from a fallen hardwood tree.

Her body convulsed with sobs. With her hair swinging wildly, for a few minutes she danced round and round the cleared flat area. It was a wild, primitive, defiant outpouring of feeling.

Then Nika sat. Inconsolable grief tore at her heart. She was aware many other mothers also grieved.

Some have probably lost more than me. But... Michael and Tom — both of them,

The knife-edged pain seared her heart and soul.

She screamed – a drawn-out desperate cry – like a wounded animal. The treetops reverberated with sound. Crows, parrots, kookaburras, and magpies shook tree branches as they soared skywards.

'Why? Why? Why? Why *both* of them?' She screamed again. The pain and passion of a mother's desperation caught and remained somehow trapped on the wind in a void of space and time.

'Why oh why?' The caught refrain carried in the wind and moaned towards the distant mountain ranges. 'All I ask is that one day someone will know where they are.'

Through the portals of time, this desperate cry would continue to echo on this hilltop.

A golden-haired child dancing here, with her dog, will one day – ninety-seven years in the future – hear, feel, and long to understand this desperate cry of love and longing, inexplicably trapped by the wind. She will be certain it needs to be resolved.

Nika's heart raced. Her passion was unabated, but she tried to pray.

'Oh, God! Tom has no doubt You are there. Help my unbelief at times like this. May indeed their spirits truly soar free, but, Lord God, I ask that one day You will guide someone to find their bodies so they will not be lost forever.' The thought their bodies could be lost and their whereabouts unknown was too hard to bear.

She sobbed wildly. 'Oh, God, give us the Strength to live on.'

Grief lasts the whole of life, but the storm today of passionate outpouring eventually abated. She remained seated for a long, long time, quiet and very still.

The breeze continued to caress the treetops. The birds returned and settled. A kookaburra laughed – the territorial cry rang poignantly clear in the morning air.

Nika's thoughts of her mother came unexpectedly. Drifting gently on the wind, she saw again the coal-black eyes and felt the eternal comfort of her Aboriginal mother's love. 'One day, darling, all will be well.'

She sighed. Then, straightening her skirt, clipping her hair back with the comb, she slowly walked down the winding road to where Tom waited.

He tended a roaring campfire. Two chairs were placed together side by side.

Logs blazed with vivid red fire, and sparks danced in the sunlight. 'Cup of tea, darling?' he asked gently. She nodded and accepted the mug. They both had the silent understanding of acute shared pain. Comforted, together they watched the life in the embers, as the log disintegrated in the flickering campfire flames.

Tom was clearing the tangled undergrowth from the edge of the dam when one of the horses in the fenced enclosure stamped a hooved foot and whinnied loudly.

Tom looked up. 'Beth? Maree?' A horse and sulky manoeuvred between the trees and gently came to a stop beside the hut.

Two figures in blue and green gingham dresses with matching bonnets leapt out. 'We haven't come to disturb your holiday.' Beth ran into Tom's open arms.

'We came to bring you something.'

Nika emerged from the hut. 'It's good to see you.' Smiling, she joined them.

Maree held a green plant carefully wrapped in a calico bag. 'It's a Moreton Bay fig,' she said as she passed it to her father. 'Jake Carruthers rode into town from Imbil. His dad said maybe you'd like to plant it here. These trees live a long time,' she added. She looked at her parents' faces, hoping their visit had not disturbed this necessary time.

'We will be going back home later,' Beth added. 'Eliza and Robert are taking a group of young people tonight to the dance in the Monkland Hall.'

How grateful I am for the continued love and support of my wonderful foster family. Nika's thoughts raced. *I wonder if they've had any news about Matthew.*

(Matthew Barritt, Nika's younger foster brother, had enlisted in the AIF Australian Imperial Forces in the same week as her sons.) Notice was received stating Matthew had been 'injured in action'.

As if understanding her mother's thoughts, Maree suddenly interjected, 'News about Matthew has come through. He's in a London military hospital. Apparently, he is going to be OK.'

Nika and Tom exchanged glances. *Maybe there will be good news after all about Michael and Tom Jr.*

Tom, Nika, Beth, and Maree planted the Moreton Bay fig at the corner of the property that same afternoon.

Many months later in 1918, when the official notification came that both boys were 'missing presumed dead', Tom added a simple plaque scratched with a nail.

Michael and Tom lost in WWI 'spiritually free to soar'

Tom, Nika, Beth, and Maree.

When Erin visited with three-year-old Michael, she added... 'Erin.' The long scratch mark that went halfway around the trunk of the two- foot-high sapling was the child's addition. He imitated his mother, and when she said, 'Daddy,' he looked at her, his blue eyes questioning, and repeated, 'Daddy.'

CHAPTER XVI

Lifetime Adventure – Lost in History

'This is the adventure of a lifetime.' A joyful refrain resonated on the hearts and in the minds of thousands and thousands of young men. It was frequently voiced in times of 'mateship' and on stopovers and training facilities in strange and foreign lands.

From nations across the world, enemies and allies alike, it was the young whose souls burnt with flames of preparedness to fight, to bring forth what they believed would be 'better' for their country and their families.

From Australia, they left the red brown plains of the inland, remote properties, and towns in some of the loneliest places on earth and joined up with ones from major capital cities and green coastland lands. They all left their homeland and journeyed into the unknown with confidence and patriotic pride.

For most, the adventure quickly changed into a glimpse of hell. The Daniels brothers were only two of the tens of thousands who journeyed, who would be 'lost in history'.

The brothers met up briefly on deck as the *Star of England* made her way across the Indian Ocean to Egypt.

'This *is* the adventure of a lifetime,' Tom remarked to Michael as the white waves creamed along the side of the troopship. 'I'm happy we can share it together.'

The flotilla of thirty-six vessels left from Albany in Western Australia in early November 1914. For all the young men, memories of home, families, and the green fields or red dust of the open plain country were swamped by ocean vastness and the thrill of unknown possibilities ahead.

A complicated operation and tight security had blanketed most of the departure details. Line after line of ships laden with men and horses had to take up allotted positions and form into a compact convoy before sailing into the open sea. The transports were escorted by the HMAS *Melbourne*, HMAS *Sydney*, HMS *Minotaur*, and the Japanese battlecruiser *Ibuki*.

After a few nights at sea, Tom was restless. The unfamiliar constant motion of the sea, and being confined constantly with so many other people, suddenly stifled him. He climbed and positioned himself behind a bulkhead, to breathe in a bit of fresh air.

He saw flashes on the distant horizon.

Gunfire… a battle? Thoughts raced. *Is it the enemy or one of ours?*

When he spoke to Michael a few days later, Michael commented, 'All top secret, brother, but there are rumours. Apparently one of our escorts, the HMAS *Sydney*, had to leave the convoy on a mission. She came back with quite a bit of damage. A battle has obviously taken place. There is also talk of a "beached" German raider ***** and POWs being taken back to Australia and some travelling with one of our ships on to Egypt.'

The two young men knew idle speculation and gossip was dangerous. This incident was never mentioned again. Tom kept the image of distant gunfire as a reminder of the responsibility of their journey ahead.

The Daniels boys sailed on into history, and like thousands of others, much would remain hidden for decades. Perhaps one day it will *all* be revealed in entirety. Only 'snippets' of this life can be played out.

On the peninsula where courage, death, and dying was an

actuality, amid the carnage of human suffering, incredible noise, and mayhem, a battle raged continuously. The army faced incredible odds in a place where there was to be no winners.

At the height of a barrage of gunfire, Michael suddenly was sure he heard Tom's voice.

'Michael! Michael! Mikey, can you hear me?'

Carefully Michael looked around. Training and instinct honed him to his surroundings, and he held his rifle ready and concentrated on the faint, familiar voice he heard above the battle noise.

He followed the sound and dropped into a trench. In a pool of squelching mud, with blood splashes staining the ground around, Tom lay. His body was an unnatural twisted shape. He smiled when he saw Michael kneel beside him, though his face was splattered with mud and blood dripped down his cheek from a bullet hole in his forehead.

'Tom! Oh, Tom!' Michael's heart splintered, and shock shuddered through his body.

Tom reached for Michael's hand.

Tenderly and gently, Michael stroked his brother's face and closed his eyes. He held his hand until he knew with certainty Tom's spirit had begun its eternity journey.

'Goodbye, my little brother!'

Beneath his khaki slouch hat, his dusty perspiring face was streaked with a deluge of tears.

He rocked back and forward in a paroxysm of overwhelming grief. 'My promise to you this day is that I will fight on. I'll do my duty as a soldier, but in memory of you, and our lives with our family, I will comfort others on the way, wherever and however I can.'

O God, give me courage and Divine Strength. Amen.

C H A P T E R XVII

Peace – Moving Forward

Gympie 1918

November:

Monday evening, the eleventh, an explosion of sound shattered the quiet stillness of the evening. The time on the mantlepiece clock said 8pm. Nika knew instantly it was the alarming clang of the fire bell in the street.

'Something's happened,' she called to the others.

Erin woke Michael. He protested loudly. She soothed him as she wrapped him in a light blanket and followed Nika, Beth, and Maree outside.

'Victory! Peace!' Cries resonated as church bells chimed, and steam whistles screamed. 'Peace at last!'

A jubilant throng headed for the town hall where the mayor announced, 'Peace has officially been declared!'

The crowd went wild.

Rousing cheers were given for the empire and all the brave defenders. The city band began playing patriotic songs. For most of the night, relief spilled over into a time of gratitude and celebration.

When Tom arrived home, he was breathless from rushing. He was relieved to see the family preparing for bed.

'I heard the news on my way back from the Ramsays' property. A stockman I met on the road kept repeating, "It's finally over! It's finally over!" He didn't even say hello!'

'I'm glad you're all home. It's good to see you and to be able to say good night.'

Good-night responses came from the girls already in bed.

Nika emerged from the doorway, gave him one of her radiant smiles, then embraced him warmly. He kissed her and murmured in her hair, 'I reckon there's going to be a big party in Mary Street, probably an all-nighter. It'll be good to have some sleep to gain energy for tomorrow.'

'Good night, Grandpa!' Michael's sleepy voice called. 'I saw a big truck. And... and there was lots and lots of noise. They're havin' a weely, weely big party.'

'I'm coming to give you a big hug.' Tom bounded across the room and swept the little boy into his arms for a massive hug. He kissed his forehead. 'Good night, and God bless you, little man.'

He tucked the covers around the child and quickly left the room.

It took a little more time than usual, but slowly, the house on Nash Street settled into its usual quiet stillness.

Outside was pandemonium. It was probably the biggest party the community had ever known.

After 1,560 days of war, peace celebrations were planned to bring the community together. It was hoped that heavy hearts could again be challenged to hope for a better future.

The first of these public celebrations was a march to Queens Park.

There, the mayor again addressed the crowd.

'This Gympie district stood the highest for enlistment in our state.'

The crowd cheered! They waved flags and coloured ribbons. Many threw hats in the air. Children danced.

Sombrely, the mayor continued, 'We must remember also, I'm saddened to confirm, one hundred and fifty of our lads will not be coming home.'

A reflective calm followed this statement, then a deep sigh swept over the people.

'Just numbers for some,' Nika sobbed into Tom's shoulder.

They stood on the far edge of the park – a golden-haired woman, a sandy-haired man, their two daughters in pretty summer dresses, their daughter-in-law with her dark brown hair which flowed freely across the shoulders of her lace-trimmed blouse. By her side, three- year-old Michael desperately tried to take a flower from the woven plait of his Aunt Beth's hair. He jumped then squealed in frustration. It was just out of reach.

'Only numbers for some,' Nika said again. Resignation and acceptance struggled to overcome the deeply sad inflection in her voice. 'We have lost our two sons. Life will never be the same.'

Maree gently removed one of the flowers from her sister Beth's hair and handed it to her little tousled-haired, blue-eyed nephew.

Michael took the daisy and laughed loudly and joyfully. He twirled it above his head and danced, round and round. His laughter resonated, and his innocent exuberance brought smiles to many faces in the crowd.

*Returned soldiers marched, bands played, and there were displays of military precision. Mary Street was festooned with hundreds of flags, ribbons, and flowers.******

The day was a complex mixture of celebration with food, drink, fellowship, and for many always, the underlying remembrance of changed lives.

Tom's heart was stirred by the spontaneous joy of his grandson, the sorrow of his wife, the inconsolable grief inside himself, and the needs of his daughters.

'In the middle of this,' he quietly said, 'we will need to go forward with hope for not just our own lives, but for this community as well.'

That afternoon, a combined churches Thanksgiving service was held in the Olympia Air Dome. It expressed united sorrow, faith, and hope for the future.

The overflow from this service – a considerable number of people needing comfort and hope – moved along Mary Street where a second service of combined Christian faith was held that night in the town hall. All prayers were for the fallen and their families, for new beginnings and hope for future peace with growth and prosperity for the city.

CHAPTER XVIII

New Year's Eve – 1923

The Daniels family assembled in the lounge room of their Nash Street house. The mid-afternoon heat of a summer day had drained them of energy. Collapsed like rag dolls, every available chair overflowed with bodies.

The telephone's discordant jangle shattered the calm.

'Not the phone again!' Tom sighed. 'Once upon a time, people came to the door or wrote a letter.'

Friends and family had phoned during the morning.

'Happy New Year to you too, darling.' Beth's excited voice now filtered back to the listeners. 'Yes, I'll be joining you in Brisbane on the sixth of January. Of course, I'm delighted about the house provided by the Department of Railways. Overlooking the river too, it'll be a whole new adventure indeed. Love you! See you soon!'

This house will be very empty when Beth and Ben (her new husband) live in Brisbane, while he pursues his promising architectural career, and Maree joins an outback medical facility. Nika sighed deeply. Her thoughts were sad and scattered.

Beth re-joined them, flopped down on the arm of the large

92

lounge chair beside Erin, and gave her sister-in-law a brief hug.

Nika whispered, 'We're going to miss you very much, dear.' 'Oh, I imagine you and Dad will find plenty to keep you busy.'

'Michael will certainly stop you from getting bored,' Erin commented. 'If the years since the war are any guideline, there's still a lot of change to come in this place. After the short-lived plague scare, the year after the war, we've moved into some interesting times.'

She stopped then laughed. 'Because it is New Year's Eve, we start to think about past years. How about we have a charade game and try to guess some events which occurred?'

There were groans.

'No, you won't have to move anywhere. We can stay in our chairs.

For example, I mentioned the plague scare. Let's begin with that.'

She lifted her hand to her head and gave little gasping noises while pointing to invisible spots on her face, arms, and legs.

Beth laughed. 'Plague!' she intoned in a throaty spectral voice. 'It's the plague! Mercifully, it *was* short-lived.'

'Now, I've got one,' Tom said. '1921.'

He extended his arms and began to silently pretend to be flying.

Then he took an unexpected nosedive and fell back in the chair.

Beth answered first. 'The first aeroplane to come to Gympie crash- landed when its wings clipped the trees.'

Maree chuckled. 'Not a good introduction to the age of air travel. It made me think I'll happily spend my life on the ground. I'm relieved there were no injuries.

'This 1921 memory is one of my clearest,' she added.

She opened her eyes widely and said, 'Oooh! Oooh!' Then she clapped her hands and said again while shading her eyes, 'Oooh! Oooh!'

Beth said, '1921 electricity replaced gas lights. Mary Street blazed with brilliant light. It was wonderful. Because it was a winter's night, the frosty glow on the pavement and shopfronts was magical.'

'Oh! I remember that night well,' Erin interjected. 'Michael disappeared. When he finally came home, he looked at me with a huge smile and enormous sparkling blue eyes and said, innocently, "I was looking at all the street lights." He had absolutely no comprehension of the passage of time and how worried I had been.'

'Oh, there was the great street party on St Patrick's Day when we celebrated the arrival of the new Memorial Park gates. Not sure how I could illustrate that event. Maybe if I had a green hat and did a little jig,' Erin added.

'Oh yes, that was a tremendous party,' Nika said. 'When the Prince of Wales came to officially open Memorial Park on 24 May, with the new gates already proudly in place, we became suddenly no longer party people but very important and regal.'

She got up and walked up and down, swinging her skirt and curtseying to each person in turn. 'Very formal, very regal, extremely well-behaved.' She collapsed back into her vacated chair and wiped perspiration from her forehead.

'A handsome man that David, Prince of Wales. No wonder he's called the dashing playboy prince,' Maree interjected.

'Not sure if he'll make a good king though,' Tom added. 'It'll take a lot to settle him down.'

'History and time will tell.' Nika smiled from her prone position in the chair. 'We had the death last year of the Catholic priest, the one who began his ministry life in Gympie in a tin shed on the gold fields. That was a significant indication of the passage of time.'

'Yes,' Tom added. 'I knew him well. He was a gentle, kind man, and his death *is* the end of an era.'

Nika's gentle voice spoke again, with feelings. 'Back in 1868, he was very kind to my mother and father. He not only officiated at their wedding but genuinely wished them well. He was a comfort through the years. I remember with gratitude.'

Tom reached out, took her hand, and smiled. Regret still surfaced when he remembered his own prejudice in the past.

For a moment in imagination, he saw the following:

Marrangaroo, gentle, dark with huge black eyes and her father, Michael, with his Irish charm, startling flame-red hair, and black red- speckled beard, both dead when Nika was only eleven.

Tom's thoughts of the past were always tinged with sadness. *I only met them a couple of times in Mary Street. I wish now I had tried to befriend them.*

Nika, seeing the shadow on his face, smiled beamed her dazzling smile. 'No regrets now, darling. Our story has progressed beyond the things of the past.'

A sudden violent crash outside rattled the cups on the bench. Sounds of splintering timber, followed by grinding, loud yells, squeals, then peals of laughter, brought the five adults running to the door.

Michael disentangled himself from the wreckage of a box-like contraption with four small wheels, now mangled and twisted out of proportion.

Three other grinning boys emerged from bits of strewn wreckage shaking splinters from their clothes.

Ten-year-old Davey Cartcutt looked up at Tom. His face was coated with dust. A wind-tangled mop of dark curls fell in dusty disarray across his forehead. Enormous blue eyes sparkled excitedly. Struggling with a desire to laugh, he said, 'M'dad made me a cart when I was a little kid. We had a goat in a harness who pulled me around the paddocks where Dad worked with me mum. Dad called it a "billy cart". Later I used to give me younger brother and sister rides.'

'We thought it'd be fun if we all made one,' Michael said. 'Tim and Max came, and we met up at Dave's place. We made them last week, and today we tried 'em out on Palentine Hill.'

The four boys gathered together now in an excited huddle. 'It was bonzer!' one of them exclaimed.

'Oh yeah, it was,' Max said. 'We pushed off from the top together. Then it got faster and faster, and one of the wheels came off and . . .' 'It hit my cart,' said Dave. 'I started to wobble then crashed into Tim.'

Michael moved to the front. With bubbling enthusiasm, he said, 'Geez, Dad, you should have seen us. There was a bit of a bump. I hit it and spun into the three others, and we all sort of crash-landed together here in Nash Street. It was so much fun! I hope we can try it again next week.'

The four boys dissolved into helpless laughter.

Erin muttered, 'No one's been hurt – I guess that's the main thing.'

After the wreckage was salvaged and each boy carefully returned home with his bits and pieces, the drowsy afternoon reclaimed its somnolent hostages, and the house returned to stillness.

It was two minutes to midnight. The evening meal was almost a forgotten memory. Scattered cups and plates from supper now interspersed with a few glasses of drinks stood ready for the New Year celebrations.

The phone rang. 'Hi, all.' Robert Barritt's cheerful voice barrelled down the line. 'Happy New Year, everyone. I'm here with Eliza thinking of you. We're with friends on Lady Mary Terrace. They built an impromptu radio aerial. We're waiting to see if we get a connection.'

At midnight, huddled round the phone receiver, they heard first a series of crackling discordant sounds. Then a crisp, clear voice, soft at first, gradually becoming louder and louder, said, 'Hello, Gympie – Sydney here. Happy New Year 1924.' There was more static then silence, except for wild cheering from outside in the street. Tins were jangled; people shouted. The year 1924 was welcomed with great enthusiasm!

'More changes!' Tom shouted through the bedlam. 'We're moving forward. We're connected to the wider world. Radio now. Go, Gympie, go!'

Everyone laughed. They lifted their glasses. 'Welcome, 1924!'

CHAPTER XIX

1924 Letter from England

My dear Nika . . .

Nika had collected mail from the Mary Street Post Office. She was delighted to see the British stamp on a letter among others in her hand.

It was a joy to sink back in the armchair at home and let her thoughts journey across the sea.

Emily began with her usual stylish flourish and continued:

My heart remains connected to yours as you journey on, living with the loss of your two sons. My hope and prayers for you are that life will still bring promise and unexpected joys.

Here in England, life has changed considerably since the war. Many more women are working in positions formerly occupied by men. At the bank, several senior staff members have not returned. Sadly, many men who came home from the war were prevented by injuries and illness from ever working again. There are eight women in office positions and tellers where, for years, I was the only female on staff.

Have you any moving picture theatres in your town? Some friends and I saw Beau Brummell at a special hall set up especially for the purpose. Have you heard of it? (A very interesting story.)

In live theatre, all sorts of interesting people are going 'on stage'. Some chap called George Formby brought his ukulele with him and he's now popular in music halls all around England.

A comedy lady – Gracie Fields – featured in something called a 'review'. I've been told it's extremely funny. It has a peculiar name: 'Mr Tower of London'.

There's lots of talk among some of my fellow workers, who love the theatre, that a young woman, Gertrude Lawrence, will certainly make a name for herself. She's partnered with an actor/writer, Noel Coward. He wrote a musical review, 'London Calling', so she could have a part. People love her featured song 'Parisian Pierrot'.

****

Times are difficult despite the '20s gaiety and seemingly boundless confidence. Many families genuinely struggle with household expenses as the country tries to recover from all the expense and losses of the four-year war! I imagine it's the same for you down there.

We can only hope this Great War will mean peaceful years stretch ahead now for us all.

Nika, I loved your story 'Free Spirit' published at Christmas time in the 'Overseas Contributions' section of the Daily Mail. Such a beautiful glimpse of life in open air with wind-blown hair and clouds above shredding and evaporating. I hope you will always write your stories. They are a gift to others.

I should probably get back to work. I'm trying to replace

some curtains but I think I've told you before, I hate sewing! Please give Tom my love and say hi to Beth and Maree. You must have been sad when Beth and Ben decided to live in Brisbane. I hope the gift I'm sending for their new home arrives safely.

I wonder if Maree will return to a hospital nearer home when she gains wider nursing experience.

Please tell her I asked after her and give greetings to Erin and that grandson of yours you've told me is 'growing like an ironbark – tall and strong'.

I hold you all in my heart and although we have never met I believe one day someone from there will meet with me here.

Love

Emily

'Perhaps she'll come over here,' Tom commented. 'Are you going to tell her in your reply about all the "interesting stuff" happening here in Gympie?'

'Yes, and I may even hand-draw a copy of the Dan Barry theatrical/dramatic society programme from the Variety Theatre.'

'You can also tell her we went to two silent movies, *Little Rascal* and *Second-Hand Rose*, at the Royal in Mary Street. Stuff happens in all the big grand places, but here in Gympie we've always had "variety". Lots of the "unexpected" – not always good in the mix, but it's certainly not boring.'

He laughed, and Nika naturally moved into his open arms. They danced like happy children around the small lounge room. Sunlight streamed through the open windows, and the soft lacy curtains fluttered in the breeze.

'A letter from Emily always cheers me up.' Tom grinned.

'Me too!' Nika smiled up at him. Their shared laughter resonated around the room.

CHAPTER XX

1925 Rail Disaster – Reunites Old Friends

'It's been a wonderful challenging life,' Edward Kildark remarked to his wife, Beth, one hot January evening in 1925. 'Since our Gympie wedding in 1883, ******** we've lived in fifteen different houses.'

Beth laughed. Her blond hair was now peppered with grey, but her smile remained youthful and radiant. 'Our children were born in three different railway expansion towns. Our whole life has been packing and unpacking. Difficult, but I would never change a thing.'

'Yep, I think the 1903 Gympie flood spurred on the completion of many lines. Even the war only slowed it all down for a couple of years. I reckon Rob Barritt, in Gympie, will have a massive map on his wall now. Railway lines, like octopus tentacles, are spread across Queensland. In fact, Australia is so connected trains are moving folks vast distances. The whole country is developing very quickly.'

'I have a surprise!' Ed's voice rose suddenly, giving it a more excited edge. 'I have been given two weeks' holiday as a bonus to celebrate my more than forty years with Queensland Railways. I have tickets on the Rockhampton Mail train for 8 June this year. They are first-class sleeper tickets. We can travel all the way to

Rockhampton and stay there for a few days and return anytime in the following week or the week after. All accommodations will be paid. We even have a short stopover in Gympie on both outgoing and return trips. We could meet up with Rob and Eliza and perhaps even Nika and Tom.'

'Ed, that would be wonderful. Let's go to Rockhampton, but please phone our Gympie friends and see what we can plan for a short time with them as well.'

Eyes shining, she added, 'It's exciting. Maybe we'll be able to walk around Rocky and visit the new park they're planning up there. There must be much we can see and do.'

Eliza Barritt was excited when she phoned Nika. 'Ed and Beth Kildark will be stopping for about an hour at Gympie Station on 9th June. Please tell Tom and perhaps you both can join Rob and me to share a bit of time with them.'

'I've only seen Ed and Beth three times since I was bridesmaid at their wedding,' Nika replied, laughing. 'Yes, we'll certainly try to be there to say hello again. Just let us know the time and plan when you know.'

'It'll be early morning. That's about all I know right now. Bye, love. Take care!'

The train left Brisbane late on the night of Monday 8 June and chugged and puffed its way north through the darkness. Two powerful locomotives hauled a travelling post office, a mail wagon, four sleeping cars, four sitting cars, a baggage wagon, and a brake wagon.

An early-winter night of inky blackness, peppered with the mist-shrouded sparkle of distant stars, was cooled by a gentle breeze. This light wind teased at the tree leaves and branches as the train swept past. A trailing smoke spiral from the powerful steam engines lingered in the air.

Passengers dozed. Most in the sleeping cars were already fast asleep.

'Beth, wake up!' Edward violently shook her shoulder. 'Darling, wake up! Something sounds wrong to me. Listen!'

Beth heard somewhere behind them, a strange bumping sound and an occasional grinding noise.

They sat up.

There was an incredibly loud *bang*, followed by grinding crunching noises. The train slowed then came to a sudden jolting stop. They fell to the carriage floor from the bunk bed and landed in a sprawled heap.

'I'm OK,' Beth gasped. 'Me too.'

They struggled to their feet, grateful they were unhurt.

Ed's first view out the window shocked him so profoundly he drew Beth into his arms and held her close. Quietly he spoke in her ear. 'There's been an accident, love. It looks like two or even three carriages have toppled off a bridge into a creek bed. The sleeping cars are fine – it seems to be two sitting cars and a huge wagon, perhaps the luggage car. It's absolute carnage. One carriage has fallen on top of the other.'

A voice yelled, 'Please, would all passengers who are unhurt remain exactly where you are. You are quite safe! It's too dangerous for anyone to move until we know which doors will open on solid ground. Your carriages are safe. They are on the rail line. Please stay where you are. It's too dark for anyone to be wandering around.' Ed reached into the side compartment of his overnight case and brought out a small box. The first-aid package was limited. *At least there is a torch and a quantity of disinfectant.* His thoughts raced. 'Beth, darling, please don't argue. I want you to remain here. I know you won't go back to sleep, but perhaps stay on the bunk until we know what's going to happen. I'll see if I can help in any way. I'm a member of staff, and it's my responsibility.'

'Please, Ed, don't go!'

'Darling, you know I must try to help in some way.' 'Be careful, love.'

'You too. Stay safe until you're told to move.'

Ed tentatively dropped to the ground. The thin beam of torchlight showed him that the engines, front carriages, post office, mail compartment, and all sleeping compartments were clear of the bridge. One passenger carriage was on its side smashed against the creek bank while two others were matted broken carcasses on the creek floor.

He took a deep breath, rolled up his sleeves and trouser legs, then slid down the incline of the creek bank.

Absolute carnage all right! Where can I help? What should I do first?

A pair of legs protruded from a mound of collapsed timber and twisted metal. He heard a groan.

Suddenly, a voice spoke behind him. A tall man, coated with dust with a face starkly white in the darkness, said, 'We'll have to do this together. We'll carefully lift what we can. We can do very little until help arrives. Perhaps the injured may be made more comfortable if we carefully remove what we can.' He spoke so calmly with such clinical efficiency that Ed nodded without replying.

(This passenger would later tell his tale of survival – being thrown out of an open train window. 'I got up to get a breath of fresh air.')

Together the two men worked side by side. They carefully laid four dead bodies side by side in a flat area and comforted a seriously injured young man who had been pinned beneath the rubble.

A ringing telephone's noise pierced the dream. Tom struggled to bring his consciousness back from the beauty of his galloping horse and the wind blowing through the horse's mane and teasing at his hat. 'Hello,' he said. His voice was slurred and indistinct. 'Hello.'

'Tom? Rob here. Sorry to disturb you, mate, at this ungodly hour. Disturbing news has just come in. Apparently the Rockhampton Mail train has derailed somewhere just north of Traveston near Tandur. It sounds very serious. I'm afraid I don't have any other info. An ambulance, six doctors, and seven nurses from Gympie will be dispatched. They're expecting lots of injuries and even fatalities.' His voice faltered. He struggled to speak clearly. 'The info is very vague. Will you come? I'm taking the car.'

Tom, fully awake now, glanced at the clock: 2.30am. 'I'll ride out,' he said simply. 'I'll bring the dray in case there's anyone or anything needing transport or help with cartage.'

Oh, God. Thoughts came flooding back. *The last time a dray was used at a railway accident, it transported the injured and later the dead. Please, Lord, if the news is bad about Ed and Beth, we'll all need Your Strength and Grace. Amen.*

'I'll tell Nika then head straight out. Rob, please take care.'

Tom dismounted at the accident site. He freed the horse and parked the dray.

His gaze swept over the shattered mess in the creek bed. His heart sank.

He stopped and stood completely still.

Father, help me. Amid the sadness and pain, use my hands and my abilities to be comforting and useful. Amen.

A man clutching the hand of a young girl appeared out of the darkness, in front of Tom as he slid down the bank.

'She's dead! She went to the toilet, and now Julie's dead.' The man's voice was high pitched and frantic.

He staggered. Tom caught him. 'Mate,' he said gently, 'let's go and sit over there.' With one arm across the girl's shoulder, he steered them both to a slightly raised flat area on the gully incline. Soundlessly he held them both as shuddering sobs wracked the man's body, and the child cried, making hardly a sound, as tears coursed down her cheeks and dropped on the grass.

Thick darkness still enveloped the scene, but as rescue teams and medical help arrived, pinpoints of light and moving human shapes were suddenly everywhere. A medical aide shepherded the man and child into an improvised aid tent on the bank opposite the bridge.

Tom now joined a group of men as they reverently, with great care and sensitivity, placed the bodies of the dead side by side away from where the injured and the more seriously injured were being monitored to ensure lessening of pain and speed of care.

There were nine confirmed dead and one critically injured.

A further twenty-nine were assessed by a medical team when

they were cut free and removed from the wreckage.

Gympie Hospital waited in certainty that all of them would be admitted.

'Tom!' Ed and Robert materialised out of the gloom. It was an unreal moment. There was no time for conversation. A quick handshake was exchanged, then all resumed their urgent task of shifting and disposing of rubble to help the medical team in every way possible.

'Dad!' A slight figure in a nurse's uniform moved towards Tom in the darkness. He gasped. The face reminded him of one of Florence Nightingale he had seen in a book. This similar face, indistinct in the dimness, was elfin-like, swamped by enormous eyes. Splatters of blood stained her dress front and shoes.

'Dad!' she said again.

'Maree, darling. How long have you been back in Gympie? What are you?'

'Arrived only yesterday. I was going to come home and surprise you later in the week. It was my first night-time shift, and I volunteered to help. Dad!' She reached out, almost desperately, to grab at his arm. 'Will you please pray for me. Tonight has been hard. I found two dead bodies, and a young woman died in my arms.'

Tom embraced her tightly against his chest. Quietly and fervently, he prayed. He kissed her tenderly on the forehead and gently said, 'Dear one, you will be a great nurse. This experience will be the one you remember always to make you stronger.'

'Oh, Dad.' She clung to him sobbing. Then she swallowed, squared her shoulders, and added, 'I'm to go to Gympie in the ambulance with the first team. I may not be back tonight.' She kissed him. 'I love you!'

Lining up with other medical personnel, she waved as they prepared patients for transportation, grateful for private cars and a couple of old battered trucks, as well as the ambulance. Tom's dray was again used for temporary reverent storage of dead bodies.

Gradually the site was cleared. All debris was carefully sifted for personal possessions, and by 6.30am the engines and front carriages of the train, carrying passengers and a few of the injured, resumed its chugging, belching journey to Gympie.

Tom later sat with Nika at their kitchen table. 'I was incredibly proud of our community this morning,' he said. 'When word spread, folks came from everywhere. There was an army of people. Even a couple of farmers came from a house near the site, still in their pyjamas. There were vehicles, shovels, cutting equipment, first aid kits. People prayed as they worked. Services to honour the dead are planned for later in the week. It's amazing how many people on that train have come from nations all around the world. An absolute barrage of offers of accommodation and ongoing help for the injured has come in from all over town and nearby farms.'

'Where are Ed and Beth?' Nika look tired. She had been restless and walked and prayed most of the early morning until she finally heard Tom's returning footsteps at the door.

'They are going to be well cared for. Apparently ongoing passengers will be questioned in Maryborough. They want to record an account of what they may have seen or heard. Then I'm presuming the journey to Rockhampton will be normal to ensure the mail is delivered. Their holiday should go ahead as planned with extra days added to their schedule if necessary.

'Ed called out to me just as they were leaving. "Don't worry about us, mate. Everything will sort itself out. One day at a time – that's *all* any of us really can hope for."'

C H A P T E R XXI

Nika's Letter to Emily 1930

December

My Dear Emily,

Apologies for taking so long to answer your last letter. I was delighted to hear all your news and will endeavour to answer your questions. I hope you are feeling better now. Influenza is certainly exhausting and very hard to shake off.

No doubt you're hoping for a white Christmas. Here we'll be trying to enjoy the season and keep from melting. Maybe we'll keep cool under the hose before facing any cooking, etc.

Your interest in the 1925 railway accident has certainly made me think back. Yes, you are right. It was indeed a wonderful response from our hospital and help came from many places, but the team at the hospital did an outstanding job. Yes, there are many churches in this city and yes, they all in their various ways responded.

Maree did fall in love with David Kenton, the Canadian

patient injured in the accident. She nursed him for several weeks. They were inseparable and it was a sad time for us all, and she was heartbroken when he returned home.

The latest news is that constant letters 'toing' and 'froing' across the oceans have sorted out their lives. They are planning now to marry here in Gympie in the New Year and plan to live in Canada. Tom and I are, of course, sad that both our daughters will raise their families away from us. We are happy about David. He is a lovely young man and we know he will make our youngest child happy. She has even been offered a great job at a leading hospital in Vancouver. Next letter, I will tell you all about the wedding.

Last month on the 1st Tuesday I went to an afternoon tea party. Not sure if you've heard of the Melbourne Cup. It's a horse race. The very last thing I'd normally be interested in is horses racing but a horse running this year was causing a lot of interest. With the funny name of Pharlap, people were talking about him. Some said, 'He is absolutely unbeatable.' Others were quite dismissive, 'Maybe there is a slim possibility he could complete the distance.'

We listened on the wireless and Pharlap absolutely flew to the finish line. He won by three lengths. I still don't like horse racing but this horse is really something!

Oh, I almost forgot to tell you. Rob and Eliza are going on an overseas cruise in the middle of next year. They may be away for many months. It is a prize for long service with the railways. Tom and I are willing and quite delighted to be living as caretakers at Jakdawn until their return. Erin and Michael will live here in town and travel out to the Hillrock property to stay for occasional weekends.

Michael enjoys high school. Gympie has great educational opportunities for all our young folk. Gympie High School is expanding rapidly and since 1912 has provided free education and excellent teachers, with impressive qualifications. All students who have achieved a year 5 education and pass an entrance exam can attend.

Makes me realise how far the town has grown since I was a child. St Patrick's continues its proud history of educational excellence and Eliza and Rob now have four grandchildren enrolled with this Catholic education system. Opportunities and diversity... I've seen these as God's provision and purpose for us all here. Out on the properties many of the farms need the young folk to continue working the land. They may not be able to take advantage of the full educational opportunities being offered but I know for them and future generations, strong structures are clearly being put in place.

I hear Tom unsaddling in the back paddock behind the house. He rides out each day to check on widows and their families still struggling after the war to keep up with milking and maintenance on large dairies.

There're quite a few cars around now. They have changed the structure of all our streets but for now I still prefer to walk. We still have two horses, Jet and Firefly. We'll take them with us when we're caretaking Jakdawn.

Must close. Hope you had a beautiful Christmas (not sure how long this letter will take to reach you), and will feel 'restored' and challenged again by memories of the Reason for the Season.

Blessings and love to you always.

Nika xx

P.S. The page from my diary I have included with this letter is for your prayers and contemplation. I wonder if shadows from India still surface in your life. My dream was very REAL. One day, dear, someone from here will meet with you over there and perhaps what I have written will be discussed. Who knows an answer may even be found.

There's no accident about our corresponding. It's some sort of God-link. I'm grateful.

Bye for now!

The clattering of the departing train faded into the distance. Tom reached for Nika's hand. 'Just the two of us again, now.'

She buried her tear-drenched face into his shoulder. 'I don't want to be sad. They both looked radiantly happy.'

Tom nodded. His thoughts drifted back to the January wedding.

The little Methodist Church packed with people. The heat, the laughter, the certainty on the faces of Maree and David. The confidence of their emphatic responses to the marriage vows. 'I do!' 'I will!'

How proud I felt to stand beside them. Beth and Ben with their baby girl, Eliza and Rob — supportive family and wonderful friends all around us. It was a beautiful day. Travel well, dear Maree and David. May your voyage to Canada be a wonderful honeymoon and you find your new life there fulfilling in every way.

'Let's go home and have a cuppa, darling.'

He smiled, and like it always did when she looked up at him with her golden eyes and responsive and beautiful smile, his heart contracted and pounded in his chest. 'Oh, Nika, my love,' he murmured in her hair. They were laughing as they entered their Nash Street home. 'It was unexpected of Rob and Eliza to delay their trip because of Maree's wedding,' Nika commented. 'I've assured them we will stay at Jakdawn from the beginning of March until they return.'

The cloying heat, fanned by a dry, warm breeze, filled the room, but they settled comfortably together. Thoughts were still with the young couple on the train.

Ahead of them a long ocean voyage and then a new life in Canada.

'The cycle of life,' Tom said reflectively. 'Always unexpected.

Always with possibilities.'

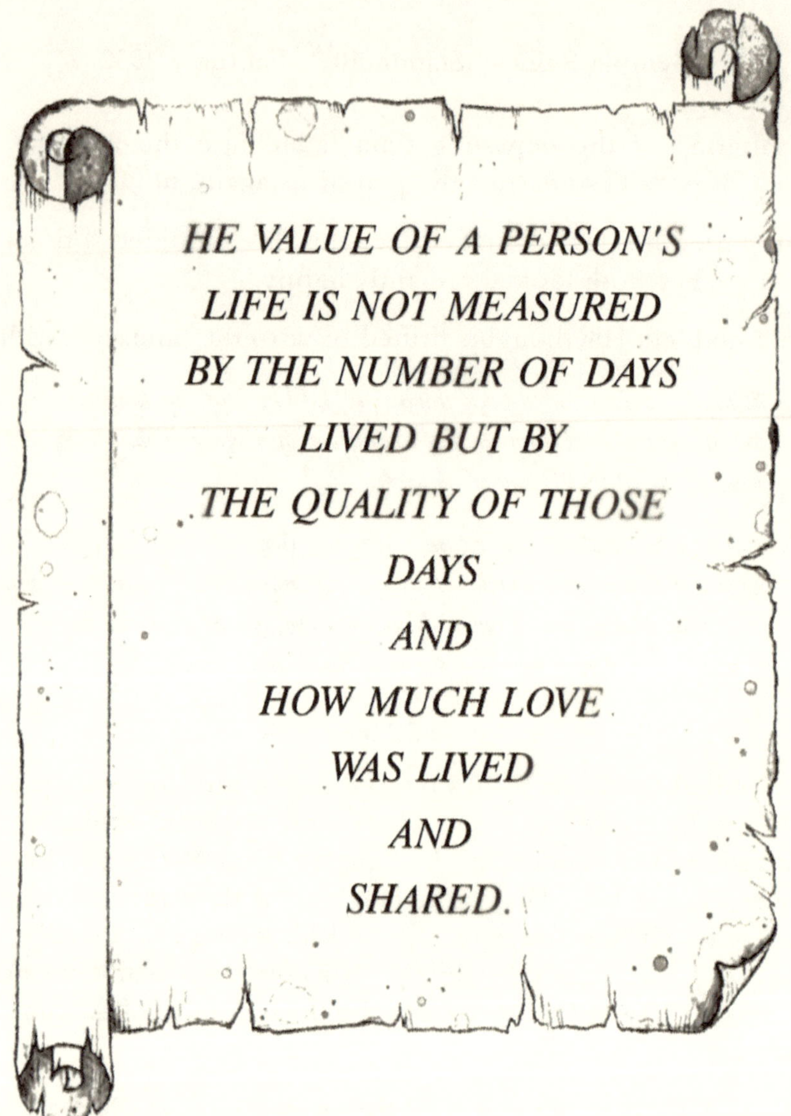

HE VALUE OF A PERSON'S
LIFE IS NOT MEASURED
BY THE NUMBER OF DAYS
LIVED BUT BY
THE QUALITY OF THOSE
DAYS
AND
HOW MUCH LOVE
WAS LIVED
AND
SHARED.

C H A P T E R XXII

Tornado

22nd September 1932

The day began, like many spring mornings, with the breathless hush of rising heat and rousing chirrups as birds prepared to sing forth welcome to a new day.

The breeze began as a gentle wind, but birds changed normal daily patterns and began a silent skywards flight, instead of their morning strident chorus.

People in town would later say it was like a 'spout', a swirling black vapour cloud, not large but with a frantically spiralling centre. This centre had bits of bark, trees, and even galvanised iron in its heart.

It picked up speed and with a short, sharp burst of energy slammed into town, leaving behind a path of destruction. It was still just after 8am, and people were already on the move. A group of Gympie High students on their way to school were thrown, unhurt, against a fence. Michael Daniels dropped his satchel and watched it bounce and roll along the street.

Monkland State School was destroyed, houses and shops unroofed, and much of Perseverance Street flattened.

It was later recorded as a 'tornado'.

For Nika and Tom, happily enjoying life at Jakdawn, it was to have been their final day. Eliza and Rob had phoned the previous evening. They were back in Gympie and would return home mid-afternoon.

The terrified bellow of the calf followed by the mother's strident calling alerted Nika to the problem.

'Tom! Tom!' she called as she ran down the bank. 'The poor little thing has fallen in the river – a section of the bank has given way.'

She charged into the river and managed to reach the struggling animal before it drifted into the faster-flowing centre current. She flung the rope loop over its head and turned it with a mighty push, back towards the bank.

Tom cheered, 'Well done, darling. I've got her now. Her mum's certainly pleased she's back on dry land.'

Suddenly, the river surged. It was as if a strong wind from the town upriver area had lifted and driven a torrent of water in their direction.

Nika was tossed around wildly. She struggled to keep her head above the lapping buffeting waves. Her sudden scream pierced the chaos.

'Tom! My foot is caught under a tree root. I can't move it.

Something heavy has wedged it tightly.' 'Hang on, love, I'm coming.'

There were wind gusts now blustering with occasional bursts of strength and speed that shredded leaves from overhead trees. These leaves floated now on the river's surface like an armada of tiny boats.

Tom frantically looked for something to pass her to cling on until he could swim out. A solid piece of fence post was all he could find to stretch across the water. At least it floated.

Everything was flowing around wildly now. He needed to get to her somehow, quickly.

The overhanging branch seemed a viable option. Tom crawled along. 'Darling, reach up, take my hand. I won't let you go.'

'Tom, it is too dangerous. You'll be swept away as well. My love, I may not be able to get free. Don't risk your own life as well.'

He reached down and grabbed her outstretched hand as the river tossed and churned and the wind howled around them.

A sudden gust. The branch broke. Tom hurtled into the swirling water. He still held Nika's hand.

He struggled to stand. It was a desperate surging, blindly groping, push against a powerful opponent. Once beside her, he wrapped his arms around her, and she held him. Her foot remained jammed tightly. She tried to wriggle and push, but it would not come free.

Tom kissed her. 'My love, I'll have to try to do something.'

He filled his lungs with air and duck-dived beneath the surface. Gently using her body for guidance, he worked his way down and found where her foot was caught.

His heart dropped.

A section of the bank has slid across the tree roots. Her leg may even be broken. It's caught under a huge rocky slab. I can't move it!

Father, hold us. Be our Strength. Amen.

He surfaced and stood again beside his beautiful wife. Loosened tendrils of her golden hair, now with grey strands intermixed, trailed and flowed across the bouncing water's surface.

He positioned himself securely at her side, held her closely, then kissed her gently and tenderly.

The water around Nika rose with increasing persistence. Tom saw tears in her eyes as it lapped now at her face.

As the river's water level rose faster and faster, the surge became stronger and more erratic.

'Look up, darling,' he said. 'Keep your eyes on the sunlight dancing on the treetops. Watch the clouds dancing in the blue sky above.' He clung to her and never once released his embracing hold.

'Tom,' softly, her voice barely a whisper, she said. 'Darling, I… I… can see Tom and Michael.'

Together in death, as they had been in life, they focused upwards, and the water flowed over them. This river called Mary, passionately loved by them both, swept over them, and they were carried into eternity.

Their legacy will live on. Questions one day will be answered.

Afternoon silence replaced the morning's dramas for Gympie, and for those who would mourn the passing of Nika and Tom, for them too absolute peace would one day replace the loss – when grief's storms had passed.

December 1932

London

Dear Michael

My heart felt like it would break when I heard the news of your grandparents' deaths. Nika and Tom have been part of my life from a distance for many years. I will forever treasure my memories of Nika and her wonderful writing gift.

To you and your mother my heartfelt condolences as you work through this time of deep grief. I know what they both would want is that you fix your eyes ever FORWARD to what is the goal and purpose of your lives.

My life, my home, any resources I may possess will ever be open to receive you.

I live in the Hope that one day a personal 'connection' will be forged.

Prayers are being said here for you all. We share your grief but also give thanks for the lives of your grandparents and their rich legacy of faith and love.

Emily

THE PAST
AND THE PRESENT MEET

Graves Discovered

Mysteries Unravelled

CHAPTER XXIII

Passionate Quest

**Why spend years looking for a burial site that might
not exist?**

Lambis Englezos

Searching for the *missing*

All direct quotations used in this chapter are courtesy of archival records.

*Cite: Lambis / wartime 44 (2008) 6–17 (wartime/44.index` My Quest to
find the missing`.asp)*

After the wartime tragedy at Fromelles in 1916, 1,335 Australians
were missing.

All Australian and British soldiers killed behind German lines had
been gathered and buried. It was high summer, and with the
desperate need to clear their lines, the Germans had a huge
collective burial pit dug. Numbers were recorded; wherever possible,

116

ID discs and personal items were bagged then sent to soldiers' families through Red Cross.

(Erosion and the vagaries of warfare meant, however, that many died in pockets of remote bushland.)

This recording process is to be commended. Numbers recorded equated almost exactly with the numbers buried. Only modern advances in DNA identification could ever unravel and bring individuality back to those soldiers and others buried in more obscure places.

It certainly did not happen instantly. It took many years of painstaking research, working with governments, combing through thousands of army records, and talking with veterans' families and army authorities. There was also furious opposition about disturbing the dead and the certainty of others that with absolute respect the missing must be identified wherever possible. Families must be given this gift of 'answers' and 'closure'.

Pheasant Wood in Fromelles was a constant theme in Red Cross records and books of military history. The searches in the late 1920s had not revealed any massive grave, yet the precise details found in a German document dated 21 July 1916 two days after the battle was a confirmed piece of the puzzle. *For us in 2002, a team GUARD, from Glasgow University, using a lot of clever technology concluded 'this site is of interest'. They uncovered two Australian emblems after a cursive surface scan.*

Madame Demassiet in a later generous gift donated all the land, and Martial Delebarre and the people of Fromelles will now be forever custodians of Pheasant Wood and the land which Madame Demassiet proclaimed 'belongs to the soldiers'.

Gallipoli Missing

One of the last surviving Gallipoli veterans in 2002 told a nurse, 'I know all the young chaps who fought and died are there. Gallipoli trenches extended far into the banks. They've caved in and become overgrown, but they are there. *Tell 'em to keep lookin'.*'

Tremendous efforts continued to be made by civilian scientists and archaeologists. Gradually unravelling of the past on the Gallipoli Peninsula, in Fromelles and Pozieres, happened, and individual stories unfolded.

CHAPTER XXIV

Hillrock… Gympie 2015

The New Year came in with a surge of climatic unrest with stormy skies and days of high temperatures.

Max hated hot weather. His coat had been clipped, and he resembled now a shorn sheep. His tail was still a plume of impressive black and white border collie with silky hair, but his body looked a pinky/grey colour.

'I know it's hot, boy,' Peter said as he scratched behind his ear. Delighted, Max pranced round and round the man seated in the cane chair in the verandah shade.

Peter remarked to Grace as she came through the door and sat beside him. 'Age has its blessings, but sometimes I'm finding, like Max, this summer heat is getting a bit harder to take.'

'I'm having trouble moving from the chair sometimes,' Grace replied.

'Even when I do, I collect what I need and sit down again. I'm blaming the heat but… perhaps, it's really a lack of motivation.'

'Aw, it's too hot to be motivated!' They looked at each other,

119

nodded, and laughed.

The telephone rang. Max barked excitedly from his position under Grace's chair. No one wanted to move.

It was the landline. 'I had to get you guys on the clearest connection possible.' The voice of their grandson Lachlan reverberated down the line. He sounded excited, distant, but clear. 'My mobile works fine, but I know you both have trouble with yours sometimes. You're still in that black spot where signals tend to come and go. I'm in Turkey. I'm here with a small group of international observers. Today, they have begun positive identification of several bodies recently discovered in a rocky alcove in the hillside here in Gallipoli. Remember when I texted at Christmas I asked for family names. Well, authorities in research matters put Sandilands and Daniels on some sort of database. Results came back today for a Graham Sandilands and a Tom Daniels. Are these relatives of ours?' Peter swallowed and choked back tears. 'Graham Sandilands was my grandmother's missing younger brother. She grieved for him her whole life. "We'll meet again one day," she used to say. If this is positively confirmed, son, it's the most wonderful news. To know where someone is buried, even if you didn't know them, is good news.

'Grace, can you come to the phone, love? Our Lockie has some information about Gallipoli missing soldiers.'

Grace stood beside him. They angled their bodies to catch a breeze from the open window.

'Was Tom Daniels a missing soldier in your family, Gran?'

'I know for certain a Tom Daniels was mentioned by my father as a dearly loved grandfather, but I don't remember hearing that his father was also called Tom. My grandmother Erin kept her private life and sorrows very personal. Yes, Lockie,' she said, after a few moments of private reflection. She nodded. 'Yes, I'm pretty certain Tom Daniels is my missing grandfather.'

Max got up and nuzzled her hand. He sensed something different in her tone of voice.

Lachlan's excited voice came again. 'I felt certain about Tom when Gympie came up beside his name in ancient army files now in internet storage. Records are being released – something about a sixty-year ban on personal files being lifted. Among Tom's belongings they found an engraved disk like a flattened penny. It reads, "Tom – little brother." On the reverse, "Love, Micky." So they're looking now for a Micky or Michael Daniels. Records list both brothers as missing.

'I'll have to go, but I'll keep you both in the loop if I have more news. The search for Michael will continue here. For now, I'm certain the information I've been given to pass on is accurate and verified.

'I hope my mum and dad will come to realise I'm not wasting valuable time by taking a year off uni to come to work here. They freaked out about Thailand. Turkey must have blown their minds. Catch you guys later. Luv yah! Bye.' The line went suddenly silent.

Grace and Peter embraced. 'How amazing!' They did a little jig, and Max forgot all about the heat and his age. He circled them, prancing excitedly and giving little barks.

'OK, fella, here's what we'll do. A little bit later we'll all go for a walk, and maybe, just maybe, you'll get to have a swim in the dam before dark.' It was uncertain if the dog understood, but his bright eyes looked at Peter with intelligence, and his excited circling became wilder and more exuberant.

They returned to their verandah chairs. Max again stretched out, this time beside Peter with his head cradled on the elderly man's sandaled foot.

A cooler breeze blew from the distant ocean and brought refreshment and peace.

'I wonder,' Grace said quietly, 'will they find Michael Daniels at Gallipoli?'

'I'm certain now they've begun, they will try to locate all the missing.'

Is this destined to be the year in history when many mysteries affecting countless families will be solved?

CHAPTER XXV

Connections and Revelations

Hillrock

'Hello, am I speaking to Mrs Grace Sandilands?' an unfamiliar voice enquired.

'Yes,' Grace tentatively replied. 'How can I help you?'

'My name is Steven Williams. I teach history as part of the curriculum at Gympie South State School.' Steven shuffled to make himself more comfortable in the straight-backed office chair. He brushed a wayward strand of dark red hair from his forehead. 'My class has been doing research for a project on Gympie's historical past. Please call me Steven, by the way.'

'Yes. Steven. Now, how can I help you?'

'Mrs Sandilands, were you Grace Daniels before you married?'
'Yes, I was and please – call me Grace.'

'Was your father Michael Robert Daniels, and did he attend school at Gympie High?'

'Yes, to both questions. In fact, many years later, I also went to

Gympie High. May I ask why you are so interested?'

'Well, in my class this year is a young lad, Luke Barritt. He can trace his family back to 1880. He found a link to a Nika O'Reilly Barritt through articles she had written. Apparently, she was adopted into the Barritt family in 1881. Nika's trail was lost after the 1893 flood, but the name Nika Daniels began as a byline in articles written in the *Bulletin* in the 1900s. We're trying to find out if Nika Daniels is, in fact, a relative of yours.'

Steven heard Grace's sharp intake of breath and knew his question had surprised her.

'It could well be the answer to a concern and question raised by our granddaughter Lisa at Christmas time,' Grace said reflectively. 'If Nika married a Daniels in Gympie and if we can find out where and when, it could begin the process of discovery... If they had children, we would have two families with a common link. Nika O'Reilly Barritt- may indeed be my great-grandmother. I was away overseas for many years and haven't thought much about the past, but I think I'll have to do some re-thinking now.'

'I would be grateful for any help you can offer,' Steven said.

'I'll try to find out about Nika's wedding. If it was in Gympie, records from one of the early churches or even Trove Civil documents should give some clues. I'll look up what I can and phone you with any info I find.'

She wrote Steven's mobile number in her diary.

'Thank you for help, Grace. When we begin research like this, we never know where it will lead.'

He laughed. 'I reckon that's why I love history and decided to be a teacher.'

Grace commented to Peter as she walked back into the kitchen, 'The past seems to be hurtling into the present.'

It was not the past that brought the present into their lives a few days later. Their granddaughter Susan phoned. It was more like a shock but with proud, poignant overtones.

'Grandad.' Her voice was hesitant, soft, but clear. 'It's Susan. I'm glad you answered. Please give Gran my love. I wanted to tell you something.'

'Is anything the matter, love? You know I will help, if it is at all possible.'

Her voice strengthened in confidence. 'Oh, Grandad, much has happened very quickly. I feel like I've been on a roller coaster. Your prayer and some things in my life appear to have been connected, and confirmed. I told you at Christmas time about my friend Tanuka and how I wanted to go to Vanuatu with him.'

'Yes, dear, I remember your uncertainty.'

'In late January, he went. I made the decision to stay. I went back to college. I found it hard to settle. I felt restless and unhappy. Did you hear about Cyclone Pam?'

'Indeed, we did. Both Gran and I were deeply concerned for the people. It was a massive storm. It made the news on all channels for several straight days.'

'It hit Vanuatu full force. Pentecost Island where his family lived was demolished. It was almost as if it had never existed. All the infrastructure went into the sea. He sent me a text before all communication was lost. I suddenly knew, I knew with a strange forceful peace and determination, I was meant to be with him. Somehow together, maybe in just a small way, we were to help and perhaps make a difference.

'I told a few friends, and suddenly, from all over, offers of financial support, assistance with airfares, and personal health needs came from many places. It was like a series of miracles, one after another. I'm leaving tomorrow to join Tanuka and Relief Aid International and will probably be away for three months. Poppy, when I told you about going to Vanuatu with Tanuka, I had no idea it would be under circumstances like this. I believe now, it is meant to be, perhaps even part of a plan.'

'I agree,' he answered gently. 'Please tell us if you have any other personal needs. We can certainly help. Grace, can you come to the phone please, dear, it's Susan.'

When he felt her figure beside him, he said, 'Susan, your gran and I stand here together, assuring you of our love and prayer support in *all* circumstances. You are dear to us. We want the best for you always. May this journey be in the Will of God and anointed by Him so you know forever you accomplished a purpose He had intended.'

Grey heads bowed, they said, 'Amen.'

Susan responded, her voice broken by tears, 'Amen! Thank you. I love you! Bye for now. Catch up with you again real soon.'

'Like a coffee, love?' Peter asked. 'Much is happening this year, we need our quiet sitting times. I'll give Cathy and Rick a ring later. I hope they're OK now about their daughter and this overseas trip. It's always incredibly hard for parents to give their children roots of stability, but also the wings of freedom to fly. My heart aches for them.'

Max wasn't sure why his human family looked so serious, but he happily joined them outside where it was cooler. Once again stretched out, head pillowed on a human foot, he was content. Being close made this dog happy in any day, under any circumstances.

CHAPTER XXVI

Heritage – Legacy – Michael

Grace's research into Nika's marriage led her to a couple of surprising discoveries. She collected all the relevant data and faithfully compiled it then passed it on to Steven Williams. She had no idea where her contribution would lead in the unravelling of the past.

'Hello, Mrs Sandilands, my name is Bernadette Barritt. Luke is my young brother. Mr Williams is his history teacher. I attend St Patrick's High School. I hope I'm not phoning at an inconvenient time.'

'Hello, Bernadette. No, dear, it's a very quiet afternoon here. How can I help you?'

'Oh, Mrs S – I hope you don't mind me calling you that.' 'No. That's fine, love.'

'Mrs S., I have some really interesting and exciting news for you. I'm truthfully a bit disappointed that Nika O'Reilly Barritt is only in our family by adoption. She is in yours by marriage and legacy. She was an amazing woman.

'Your discovery that Nika married Tom Daniels in St Patrick's Church in 1892 caused a lot of excitement at my school. Luke and

126

Mr Williams gave me your information. Confirming the marriage completed their particular area of interest. Nika was unusual for her day. References in 1900s archival biographies describe her as beautiful and artistically talented.

'We discovered her father was an Irish immigrant who took out an early mining lease on the banks of the Mary River. Our research petered out in the 1893 flood, but at my school, we have been researching church history. Information that Nika married Tom in 1892 gave a valuable clue.

'A search of local Gympie church history only recently carefully preserved and recorded online has revealed early marriage documents. In there, the 1892 marriage of Nika and Tom Daniels was confirmed, but looking even further back, we discovered in 1869, a Michael Patrick O'Reilly married Marrangaroo. There is no recorded information about the bride. Our parish priest believes she must have been a native Aboriginal woman. Nika O'Reilly was legally adopted by Rob and Eliza Barritt, but the child's nationality was not entered.'

Grace gasped. 'Whew, what a stir that early marriage must have caused in her day! Oh wow! My great-great grandmother came from a family here even before gold was discovered. That's going to take a bit of getting used to.'

Bernadette continued, 'That's only part of why I'm phoning today. The rest of my news is even more exciting. They've found Michael Daniels's body at Fromelles in France.'

'How? What? Who? How do you know that?'

Bernadette's voice rose. Excitement caused her voice to tremble. 'Mrs S... Mrs S. My, my friend Tim Jensen, a former St Patrick's student, is with an organised team of research observers watching the recovery and identification of recently discovered bodies in ancient battle fields in France and Turkey. He texted me today.'

MICHAEL DANIELS CLEARLY IDENTIFIED. DIED 1916 FRENELLES FRANCE. FULL DETAILS AVAILABLE TO FAMILY MEMBERS COURTESY OF AUSTRALIAN ARCHIVAL RECORDS AND THE CO- OPERATION OF FRENCH/AUSTRALIAN CO-OPERATIVE HISTORICAL

'I will give you the code number so you can go online and print out the full details yourself.'

Grace wrote the number down as it was dictated.

'Thank you, Bernadette, and my sincere thanks to your friend as well.'

'It's OK, Mrs S. I'm happy, very happy that Nika had a life, and a legacy, and we have found her missing sons.

'Oh, Tim confirmed the DNA of Michael perfectly matches Tom in Gallipoli. They're definitely the Daniels brothers from Gympie.

'Before you go, Tim said to tell you the recovery of Michael's body and his possessions changed – he couldn't explain it – the hopeless, sadness of what they were uncovering. He said *read it and imagine the impact on all the tired, sad people there.'*

The girl and the old lady separated by distance and age felt now a strong connection. They said their goodbyes, reluctantly. 'I'll make sure we all meet up again soon,' Grace added. 'Goodbye for now.'

Peter and Grace tapped in the coded enquiry and watched their computer turn a blank page into a beautiful sheet of prepared information.

DISCOVERY OF ANOTHER AUSTRALIAN DIGGER
FROMELLES, FRANCE March 30, 2015

This body has been confirmed as
MICHAEL DANIELS

A.I.F. GYMPIE

The body was uncovered in a rocky, collapsed trench in the area known as Pheasants Wood.

Among the remnants of his uniform, they found an identity disk with the name Michael Daniels, Army Chaplain.

On a second disk attached to the first with a metal clasp was engraved:

1 Cor. 15:54

When this mortal has put on immortality then shall be brought to pass what is written.

Death is now swallowed up in victory.

Grace sat with her head bowed. Tears trickled through her clasped hands. 'Such long-ago sorrow. Now, joy and gratitude for past revealed and information received.'

'This legacy shatters our 2015 world where faith is lightly passed off as a "take it" or "leave it" commodity,' Peter commented. 'Thank God for believers. They know our God is not only eternal but is a God of Presence and is with us generation by generation.'

Max responded to the excitement and undercurrents of human feelings around him by running around. He circled the house, round and round, in exuberant bounds.

WOOF!

His bark rattled the windows.

CHAPTER XXVII

Gossamer Links – Past and Present

December 2015

I'm happy I know who Nika was and why she might have cried here. Gran told me what she knew of the story. Nika walked on this hilltop. Did she dance here? Did Tom make the seat I'm sitting on? Did a battle happen here? A battle between grief and faith? Between hope and despair?

Thirteen-year-old Lisa was shocked by the clarity of her thoughts.

Max whimpered as she absently fondled his ear.

'Nothing's wrong, boy. I'm not sure what I should do. I feel I want to do something.'

The trees whispered as wind caressed their leaves. The sky above was the softest blue. Only a few small white fluff balls of clouds gently drifted by.

On impulse, Lisa removed the scrunchie from her ponytail and let her hair flow free. It cascaded down her back in treacle-coloured waves infused with golden lights. Her green sundress, with the thin

131

straps, showed the slightly copper tinge on her skin.

She would never know, but in that moment, she resembled Nika like a restoration image, emerged from the distant past.

My friends can't understand why I like it here. 'You must get bored.'

'Bored! Bored? How could I ever get bored here? I love this place. I love it! I love it!' she shouted towards the sky. Birds scattered, screeching and chirping. The trees shook violently.

Max was instantly alert. 'Time for a game?' he barked and ran in excited circles.

Lisa sprang to her feet and, with hands uplifted, began to dance. She didn't know why. She danced slowly at first. The tempo of her deep inside feelings rose, then her steps became faster and faster, with the passionate abandoned freedom of youth.

The border collie's excitement became frenetic. His rapid circling increased in speed until it was as if he too danced. His plumed tail fanned like a black-and-white banner. Movements caused small dead leaves to rustle, and eddies of dust spiralled upwards.

'Nika! Nika!' the child shouted. Her voice resonated like a song. 'Prayers are answered. Your sons are no longer missing and unacknowledged. Your peace is complete. Treetops shake now and leaves rustle and move. Let it be with joy. Joy! Joy! Joy! Let life be stronger than death and Hope and Joy resonate in this place, for as long as it remains.'

Her dance slowed. Breathless, with rapidly beating heart, she gratefully collapsed into the ancient carved seat. Birds returned and slowly settled. A few continued a noisy chattering, still expressing annoyance at being disturbed.

Finally, the bush quietened. A light breeze gently fanned the child's face. Max's head nestled against her ankle. A profound and sudden peace fell over everything.

She listened. There was no more sighing in the wind – no more echoes of grief and uncertainty. For several minutes, this peace touched the child, and the dog. It was in the trees and on the grass, even in the sky. A hush – breathless, almost ethereal – enveloped them. It made movement impossible.

Then, from far, far away, a gentle sound came. Someone laughed. A laugh of purest joy. The sound travelled from the mountain and into the gorge, bounced up the hill, and settled on the ridge where the child and dog were seated. It was as soft as a breeze and the resonance clear like the tinkling of a tiny bell.

'Did you hear that, Max?' His ears were pricked, his face tilted sideways, puzzled, curious.

Several minutes ticked by in silence. Lisa *knew*. It was wisdom beyond her years. She knew a golden link, as thin and as intangible as the gossamer strand of a spider's web, had been forged. Everything, past and present, could now settle into an eternal woven cocoon of this gentle peace.

Her face was radiant. Sunlight danced in her eyes. She smiled.

Max licked her hand.

From the gorge, she heard another sound. 'Grandad must be mowing. Let's join him, and we can return to the house that way. It'll be a longer walk up the road with the mower, but we'll all be together.'

Max had no idea what she said, but one word, 'walk', registered. He barked and looked up at her with his warm brown eyes. Every muscle quivered. 'Oh yes, let's do that!'

'Hello, love.' Peter looked up at the approach of the girl and the bounding dog. Max's enthusiastic greeting was quietened by Peter's gentle hand and his loving caress to the dog's ears. 'I'm glad to see you too, boy.' Max immediately sat on his foot.

'Hi, Poppy!' Lisa smiled and kissed the old man's cheek. 'Hope you're not doing too much mowing today.'

'No, for today I'm finished. We'll head up the hill in a minute. Let's sit here on the bank and chat for a bit.' He took up a position on the low bank beside the road. Max rearranged his body against the man's leg. Lisa perched herself comfortably. They were grateful for the mottled shade from overhanging trees.

'I found something.' Peter rummaged in his overall's pocket. 'It's a bit of tin. It shone like copper in the sun, and I could see scratches cut into the surface.'

Lisa smiled as he dropped the small, uneven metal piece into her cupped hands. 'Where did you find it?'

'In the far corner of the property right near the fence line. Your Gran's father remembered a large tree which grew there during his early childhood. A cyclone blew it down. The bushfire that burnt down the hut, a few years later, also burnt right through the property and cleared away most of the dead timber. Today, I thought I'd try to mow to the corner post. The grass is growing well there this year. I disturbed a patch of leaf mould and a rock. The bit of tin shone so brightly it attracted my attention. I wiped the dirt off and put it in my pocket.'

'Pop, look!' Lisa's fingers had gently trailed across the uneven surface. 'I think there were once words here.' He bent over to see more clearly. The shifting of a patch of shade improved his vision.

'You're right, love, for a moment, I thought I saw the word "free".'

She hugged him. 'Perhaps long ago this plaque was attached to the tree. Maybe Gran will know.'

'I'm certain she'll have some information.'

'Pop, if Gran doesn't want it, please can I keep it. I'd like to put it in my box with the white rock I took home last year.

'Put it in your pocket for now, dear, and we'll sort it out with Gran when we get home.'

The expression on his youngest grandchild's face took his breath away. It was a timeless, reflective shadow, and he was affected by the certainty of her sensitivity, and this unique connection she had to the past.

She hugged him, again. 'I hope Gran knows something.'

Later, as they shared morning tea around the verandah table, Grace told them what she knew of the plaque and the tree.

'I'm very happy if you put that piece in your special box, love,' she said to Lisa. 'I'm not certain if it is a piece of the plaque. I only know there was an attachment when the tree was planted nearly one hundred years ago. Dad was sad when the remains were burnt, but my nan Erin cried. "That tree was supposed to outlive me.

Nothing lasts." I remember she wept bitterly.

'I understood then it was a memorial tree, remembering people who had died. It is very likely there was a tribute, with details and names. I think you may have found what's survived.'

'I'll take good care of it,' Lisa said. 'I believe it was very important to someone long ago. I'll respect its purpose.'

Her grandparents nodded. They saw an ageless expression of wisdom flit across her face. She gave them one of her dazzling smiles.

That night Peter and Grace sat up in bed. The bedside lamp on low bathed the room in a soft, restful glow. Grace spoke quietly, but her voice, pitched with enthusiasm, broke the night's silence. 'I had a lovely afternoon with Lisa. She told me an amazing story of her time at the high point. She has such a sensitive connection with the environment. I'm pleased she will be with us until Friday evening. Cathy and Rick are visiting for the day, and she'll go home with them at night. Young Matthew is at a camp, and Susan is still in Vanuatu. She has apparently seen lots of heartache, but her parents believe she is happy doing something she feels is worthwhile. It'll be only the three of them for their Christmas at home this year.

'Oh, Pete, don't turn off the light yet, dear. I forgot to ask you something. Marcus Barritt phoned this morning. He and Lenore are the parents of Luke and Bernadette, who researched the family history at their different schools. He asked if our family would meet with his for a cuppa and a chat about our common Gympie links.'

'I have no appointments planned before Christmas now. It would be good to meet them.'

'Tentatively, I have agreed to meet on Thursday at the Lake Alford Reserve at 10.30. There will be four Barritts and three of us. Young Lachlan's been visiting a few local schools telling kids about his trip to Gallipoli and the battlefields in France. He's surprised how interested everyone has been. It's because of the one-hundred-year anniversary I imagine. I told him where we'd be on Thursday.'

'I'm glad Lisa will still be here. I think she'll find a real friend in Luke. They both have a passion for unlocking the past.'

'They do indeed.' She laughed.

The light was extinguished. The house settled into slumber. The elderly couple slept. Lisa too was fast asleep. Her door was slightly ajar. Max snoozed in his basket and woke up with his ears alert. Nothing moved. Everything was still. Quietly he strolled down the corridor.

Next morning, a very contented black-and-white border collie was discovered, curled up at the foot of Lisa's bed.

C H A P T E R XXVIII

Meeting at Lake Alford

Gympie Last week of December 2015

Blazing summer sun sparkled on the surface water of Lake Alford. This reserve pulsates with bird life and is both sanctuary and entrance to a flourishing and proud city.

The Mining Museum and the entrance statue generate respect for mining heritage past and blend with the present happy squeals of children and family chatter from scattered, covered picnic tables and wide-open grassy spaces.

Affectionately known by locals as the 'duck pond', it remains a favourite place to visit or to celebrate reunions and other significant events. Often multi-coloured balloons flutter from picnic shelter awnings to celebrate children's birthday parties.

Standing in proud dignity, rows of white gum trees line concrete pathways which meander towards the lake and branch off, providing access points to view the marine life.

Luke Barritt ran down the pathway then shouted excitedly, 'There are little turtles here today. Bernadette, come and see before

137

they disappear.'

Bernadette joined her brother, and they walked on to the stone bridge and intently focused on the water beneath. They saw turtles, but the water also churned with the kicking feet of diving ducks and the occasional open mouth of threshing eels.

'How they all live and survive here is a miracle to me.' They looked up.

A girl in a pretty blue-and-white check shorts and top set, with a ponytail of dark golden hair, smiled at them. 'I'm Lisa.'

'Hi! It's great to meet you.' The Barritt children made space for her. The three then resumed their concentration on the rich diversity of marine life swimming beneath the bridge.

Marcus and Lenore had chosen a well-shaded table and spread a cloth before Peter and Grace arrived. Marcus's concerns that this meeting of complete strangers was going to be difficult at first were allayed when the older couple greeted them with beaming smiles and genuine warmth.

Lenore looked at Grace and laughed. 'I've seen you around at lots of places but never knew your name.'

'Same with me,' Peter said. 'I'm sure at Lady Mayoress's Command Performances in the Civic Centre Theatre, or the Gold Rush events in the street, we've blended as unknown folks in the crowds.'

'Did you both go to school here?' Grace asked. She was surprised.

They eagerly answered yes. 'Primary only,' added Marcus.

'Only secondary for me.' Lenore smiled.

Marcus continued, 'We were both born here, but life circumstances took our respective families away at different times in our lives. Lenore and I both ended up in Canberra working in government jobs. We met at a Canadian embassy function – our respective sections were volunteer catering helpers.

'We'd been dating for several weeks before we even discovered we had common beginnings. Both of us had families still living in Gympie. It was amazing! What about you, guys?'

It was Grace and Peter's turn to laugh now. 'Neither one of us was born in Australia. We were *both* born in England. We married there in 1966.'

'However,' Grace interjected; a laugh expanded her smile. 'I went to school in Gympie, both primary and high. It's my family that have the legacy heritage here.'

'Yep!' Peter smilingly continued. 'I was born in England, lived in Halifax, and my whole life was lived there, and my folks are buried there. Grace was born during the blitz years in London to an Australian father. He brought her home to Gympie in 1943, and the mysteries of how and why are only now being unravelled.'

Grace added, 'I went to England in 1965. Although it was sad to leave my dad, he insisted I had this trip away. It was his sudden death that brought us back to Gympie the year after I married Peter. In 1967, I was pregnant and didn't know until after we'd arrived here. The sorrow of Dad's death was lessened by the birth of Cathy. She is Lisa Maree's mum. James was born in '69.'

'In Gympie?' Lenore asked.

'No, they were both born in Brisbane. Peter worked for the Department of Works in Brisbane. We inherited a small home in Nash Street where Dad lived as a child, and the property, in the hinterland – our current residence. Sadly, the cottage was sold and has subsequently been built over by commercial buildings. We came to live at Hillrock in 1980 and built the house on the ridge in 1981.'

'Wow! We've all had different sorts of journeys to our forebears. It would appear they came, they stayed, they lived and died here. That's what so incredible about the story of Nika O'Reilly Barritt. She is indeed the joining link to us all in the here and now in 2015.'

Chattering animatedly, Lisa, Bernadette, and Luke joined the adults for cold drinks, chips, and cake.

'It's hot today,' Marcus commented, 'but the breeze makes it pleasant.'

A loud hail from across the park caused a sudden end to conversation. A tall dark-haired young man strode purposefully across the grass. 'Gran and Grandad,' he called out cheerfully, 'I'm glad you were easy to find.'

'It's my cousin Lachlan,' Lisa shouted. 'He's just come back from a sponsored youth trip to Gallipoli and Fromelles.'

'Oh great!' Bernadette sprang to her feet. 'Welcome, Lockie! I believe you met Tim and Julie, two past students from my school. They went as part of a student observation team.'

He nodded. 'I did indeed. It was exciting to find out they came from Gympie.'

'What an emotional and wonderful journey for you all.'

Lachlan smiled but moved directly into Grace's open arms. He looked very tired. She knew the trip, and all the later speaking and sharing must have been spiritually, emotionally, and physically exhausting.

Peter made introductions. 'Marcus and Lenore Barritt, this is our grandson Lachlan. Lachlan, Marcus and Lenore Barritt and their children Bernadette and Luke.'

A cup of coffee and a chance to catch his breath invigorated him, and then he shared. 'It's special to meet up with you all here. I'm supposed to be back in Brisbane tonight, so this break is brilliant. I'm delighted to meet up with Bernadette, Luke, and their parents. Luke, what a great teacher you must have... Mr Williams, I believe. Bernadette, your school friends were the most incredible companions. We shared some historic and significant times together. I hope we can all meet up here again. I'd like Mum and Dad and Lisa's parents and brother and sister to meet up with you guys. Did Pop tell you about Lisa's sister – my cousin Susan – and how she went to Vanuatu as part of a cyclone relief team?'

Peter shook his head. 'No, I hadn't mentioned anything about other members of the family yet.'

'Well, I heard today she and her friend Tanuka have been awarded a Red Cross Scholarship to study for a year at the James Cook University in Townsville next year.'

'Oh! That's great news,' Grace interjected. 'Sue will now feel she has a direction in her life.'

Everyone burst into spontaneous clapping. 'Good on you, Susan!'

Marcus smiled at Peter. 'It's an odd feeling, mate, you are almost old enough to be my grandfather, yet I'm strangely stirred by how our children and your grandchildren found this passion and have actually discovered by research missing ancestors.'

Peter and Grace moved round the table and smilingly encouraged the young ones to join them. Peter said, 'I think it would be great together if in our hearts we expressed thankfulness for the legacy of Limga that Nika left, also for our own life journeys, our time of meeting here, and also appreciation for this community with all the past, present, and future possibilities.'

One of the young ones finished by quietly adding, 'Amen.'

Lachlan wasn't sure if it was his cousin or Bernadette who spoke, but he smiled and gave them both a hug.

In the silence, they could hear water lapping and birds calling in the distance. Grace spoke quietly, 'Please, everyone, be comfortable for a few minutes.'

She brought an envelope from her handbag. 'I have a letter here. I was unsure about ever sharing it, but somehow the time seems to be right while we are gathered today.'

She looked at Peter. 'Sorry, love, with so much about war remembrances this year, I put it away and forgot to tell you it was among Emily's private papers.'

She paused; her smile embraced them all. Faces stared intently in her direction as she continued. 'Emily Rickards, a grand and generous lady in England, formed a deep and lasting friendship with Nika O'Reilly Barritt — I now know her as my great-grandmother Nika Daniels. Over the years, they shared many things and privately shared stories of their mothers and slightly unusual beginnings and childhoods.

'Nika wrote to Emily in 1930 and enclosed a torn page from her diary dated 24 March 1900.

'The solicitor found the letter and the torn page and included them in a box of Emily's personal papers he sent.

'He wrote a personal covering letter to me.

Grace looked at the faces all turned in her direction. 'Do you want me to read it, or would you like to read it for yourselves?

There were nods of affirmation, and Marcus said quietly, 'No, please, Grace, go ahead.'

Grace read slowly with feelings:

Dear Emily,

My thoughts wander across the ocean today. I ask have you ever had a vision/dream or moments when India and your mother's people become very real?

We have this link so I share this with you. I have a fantastic life. Tom Daniels was and is my destiny. This shadow from the past surfaced today – maybe you too have shadows from your unknown past as well. I tore it from my diary... it was written so very long ago – yet suddenly seemed REAL. I wonder what you will think.

THE DREAM

Last night I dreamt a powerful dream:

Shadowy people were camped on the river – somewhere in the past...

Through driving wind and river's roar I heard a clear voice speak –

A man separated from the mob and stood...

Black as night and tall and still...

His eyes were proud, agate hued, wide, clear and very bright...

His voice boomed out... I AM TUALA MANGAREW!

I AM GRANDFATHER... YOU ARE A CHILD CONNECTED TO AN ANCIENT, ANCIENT PAST.

I AM YOUR GRANDFATHER AND YOU, YOU, CHILD OF MARRANGAROO

YOU... YOU...

YOU ARE MY GRANDCHILD.

I do not know if this is real or fantasy. Maybe, one day, one day, someone will care enough and even be able to find out.

Love Nika

There is a comment from Emily.

When I learnt of Nika's death in 1932 I was heartbroken and felt it best to safely store the letter. I never had a chance to reply.

We had years of our wonderful friendship and rich correspondence was shared that invigorated our lives.

Please, when this is found, please, may it be

Emily.

Grace folded the piece of paper. She swiped at rogue tears creeping down her lined cheeks.

Luke spoke first. His voice resonated with excitement. 'Please, Mrs Sandilands, would you trust us to try and find out something?'

'Lisa, do you think we could research? Look for ancient files. Work with an Aboriginal researcher. Maybe Mr Williams would help as well? It could be a project – mostly done in our own time.'

'Me too! Please can I be a part this?' Bernadette spoke passionately. 'I'd like to try through some archival records at school and in my church.'

Lisa jumped up; she skipped round the table. Bernadette took her hand. The girls, one with dark hair swinging across the shoulders of her yellow/brown top and the other whose ponytail swung and caught flashes of gold from the sunlight, now danced. 'Oh, Luke and Bernadette, could we at least try?'

'Amazing, absolutely amazing.' Lenore was overwhelmed by her own rising excitement. For someone, a Barritt through love and acceptance, she has made an extraordinary impact. 'I'd like to help in any way I can.'

Marcus laughed. 'Me too!'

Peter hugged Grace. 'It would appear,' Grace quietly added, 'a rock-solid heart affinity indeed lasts forever.'

'Past and future – forever un-folding. Forever being revealed.' Peter extended his hand. Lachlan now stood beside his grandparents.

Lachlan's young voice with resonating passion said, 'Legacy – from ancient past to a yet-to-be-revealed promising future.'

No one heard the soft whisper wafting on the breeze.

'Yes... oh... yes.'

THE LEGACY OF LIMGA

Lake Alford

Many communities around this country and around the world
have wonderful histories and stories of families and achievements,
but this is our city – our family chose to live here.

I am proud of all its past – all its hill and valley experiences and
look forward with *hope* for a bright future.

Faye Roots

ENDNOTES

* **Eliza and Rob Barritt adopted Nika when she was eleven years old.'** Marranga-Limga'

** **Internet source questiawww.questia.com/ourlibrary–GympieCity-Mayor's new-robes**

*** 2012–2016 historylists.org

**** Three gold nuggets were given to the government in 1880 by Nika's father in trust for her education and future.

***** German light cruiser *Emdem*

****** *Maryborough Chronicle*, Saturday 16 November 1918

******* *Parisian Pierrot' became Gertrude Lawrence's signature tune for many years.*

******** Marranga-Limga – 'The Wedding